the TAINTED ISLE

A COLLECTION OF
DARK GOTHIC TALES BY

DAN WEATHERER

The Tainted Isle
Copyright © 2019 by Dan Weatherer

Cover, Interior & Endpaper Art
Copyright © Carl Pugh 2019

Published in November 2019 by PS Publishing Ltd. by arrangement with the author. All rights reserved by the author. The right of Dan Weatherer to be identified as Author of this Work has been asserted by him in accordance with the Copyright, Designs and Patents Act 1988.

This book is a work of fiction. Names, characters, places and incidents either are products of the author's imagination or are used fictitiously. Any resemblance to actual events or locales or persons, living or dead, is entirely coincidental.

First Edition

978-1-786365-44-6
978-1-786365-45-3 (signed edition)

Design & Layout by STK•Kreations
Printed and bound in England by T. J. International

PS Publishing Ltd
Grosvenor House, 1 New Road
Hornsea, HU18 1PG, England

editor@pspublishing.co.uk
www.pspublishing.co.uk

For Bethany and Nathan xxx
For Family

CONTENTS

PROLOGUE
1

THE MAN I WAS
19

THE DRESSMAKER'S MANNEQUIN
29

THE BLACK LAKE
37

THE INTERNMENT OF THE SAFE
51

THE SCREAMING SKULL
61

THE DEVIL AND THE HILL
71

THE HANDS OF EVIL
77

FATHER
83

THE HOUNDS OF WISTMAN'S WOOD
87

THE ABDON BOGGART
91

THE ART OF DISBELIEF
101

THE RESTLESS WITCH
105

MOTHER
115

THE PALLID ONES
123

THE SERPENT IN THE LOCH
133

THE INFANT VAMPYRE
143

AFTERMATH
153

THE SLEEPING SAVIOUR
159

THE FALLEN HOUSE
169

THE BELLS OF WEREDALE
177

THE DEATH OF A LORD
185

THE HAUNTING OF FENTON HOUSE
191

THE MAN WHO DID NOT DIE
199

THE MARK OF THE RIPPER
205

THE MAN I BECAME
213

ABOUT THE AUTHOR
217

"Pick at the threads of superstition and you shall uncover all manner of infernal shades."—Solomon Whyte, 1893

Prologue

THE WYTCHING TREE

Alverton — March 1871

Quite how I allowed myself to become entangled in the darkest practices of our time is a question I contemplate often. Suffice to say that when slumber eludes and I find myself far from home, I remind myself that the path I walk chooses me and it is not the other way around. There shall be time later for reflection, a time for remorse also, but this is not it. This is the story of how I became Britain's first investigator of the peculiar (later termed the *paranormal* by more learned men than I). So that you may fully understand the journey I undertook to become the man I am today, let me begin with the retelling of my first investigation: one which led me deep into the heart of rural Staffordshire.

✥

During earlier times, when truth and superstition made uncomfortable bedfellows, cases of suspected witchcraft were many. Any person deemed guilty of practicing witchcraft met with death. This was a sentence passed out by men who held no official office and were no more qualified than you or I to judge the merits of a criminal case. Fear held court for many years, and it is a blight on our history that so many were butchered in ignorance. Records, though scarce, estimate that between one and a half and two and a half thousand women were executed in England after being tried for witchcraft. The last official executions of suspected witches occurred in 1682 with the hangings of Temperance Lloyd, Mary Trembles and Susanna Edwards. Or so history states.

Rumours persisted of a much later execution having occurred in a small village named Alverton. Hearsay has it that a young wretch by the name of Mabel Othan, having allegedly inflicted untold misery upon the community, was hanged from an oak tree on 17th March 1783. That such a sentence be carried out over one hundred years after the last documented execution was worthy of investigation alone, yet stories persisted detailing the disappearance of individuals from the area around the anniversary date of Mabel Othan's execution.

I had been compelled to discover whether there was any truth pertaining to those rumours in a bid to end the tittle-tattle once and for all. Young, headstrong and with an adventurous spirit, I naively assumed that I could find fame and fortune by dispelling the myth behind the Wytching Tree.

My journey south passed quickly, and the haze filled skies I had long associated with home gave way to a bright azure. Here was a quiet I had seldom imagined possible. Save for the clatter of the horses' hooves and the intermittent squeal of the carriage wheels, there was little else to hear. I noted that what few examples of wildlife I observed did not flee from the sounds of my approach, but remained still and silent, watching my carriage as it passed them by. This quiescence ought to have unnerved me, though inexperienced as I was, I paid my surroundings little attention. In later years, I would recognise this quiet as the warning that was meant.

The majority of Alverton sits above a massive valley which slices through the heart of the county. The valley is flanked on either side by a wall of close, impenetrable forest. I was informed by my driver that the ravine's floor lay some several hundred feet below. I leaned out of the window as we passed over a narrow precipice, the carriage rocking violently from side to side as our wheels tumbled over the loose rock, and strained to see for myself. The base of the valley was hidden from sight by a thick carpet of lush treetops. I ordered the driver to stop, and for a while, he and I sat together and admired the scenery.

This was a vista like no other I had ever encountered. One grows accustomed to an ordered horizon, one lined with rooftops and tall chimneys. Here, perched on the edge of the drop and surrounded by dense woodland, I felt that for the first time in my life I was able to breathe. It was a heady mix—the combination of the scenery, the purity of the air, the steady babble of the River Churnet and the confident shouts of the loggers at work deep within the bowels of the valley flooded my senses. I experienced there a moment of serenity that I shall never forget.

My driver went on to explain that a small section of the village littered the valley floor and that further to the west, a mile into the vale, lay the neighbouring village of Oak Moor.

My lodging for the night was a coach house by the name of Swallow's Pass. The building rested on the lip of the valley and afforded a similar view to that of my earlier vantage point. Later, when shrouded in darkness, the forest cut a grey and silent shape against the matte of the night sky. Absent the day's toil, only the whisper of the trees remained.

As I made my way from my room towards the area of the tavern that served as a public house, the air carried an array of voices, all of which were engaged either in excited conversation or raucous argument. I pushed open the door that separated the guest quarters from the bar, expecting the fervour to rise in volume. Instead, a hush fell over the room, and all eyes turned towards me. An atmosphere of suspicion hung between us, the revellers and I. The moment mercifully passed. The hush broke, and a low murmur of chatter resumed. Perplexed and feeling more than a little uncomfortable, I ordered an ale and took a seat at the bar. The publican was a rotund fellow with dark eyes and a ragged beard. His face wore an expression of forced welcome and he muttered only minimal thanks as I paid for my drink.

I took a sip and gathered my composure. I was a visitor to this place, unfamiliar, an unknown quantity. If the rumours held any semblance of truth, then it was only to be expected that the community would view my intrusion with a degree of suspicion. As I drank, I felt eyes on my back. Anxious, I shifted my attention from the crowded bar behind, back towards the barkeep. It was he who spoke first.

"So, where are you from then, eh?"

I replied that I was from Manchester.

"City boy, eh? What brings you 'ere then?"

I paused for a moment. I wondered whether it would be wise to reveal my actual intention this early in the investigation. Wet behind the ears as I was, I elected to lie.

"Outsiders don't come here for fresh air. Can't even remember the last visitor we 'ad. Can you?" Though it was clear that the barkeep was addressing somebody to the rear of me, his eye remained locked with mine.

"No, I canna," came a mumbled reply from far behind.

He leaned across the bar and repeated the question in a tone laced with threat. "So…I'll ask again, sonny. What brings you 'ere then?"

I was about to reply in truth when a sudden chill took my bones. A chorus of gasps erupted behind me. Instinctively, I turned on my stool, expecting to see one or more of the local folk standing directly behind me, their patience at my intrusion having finally worn thin. As I turned, the fire that had been burning upon my arrival sputtered out, throwing much of the tavern into darkness. Silence fell upon the bar, and a tangible feeling of dread permeated the air. All at once the fire burst into life, only this time, the flame burnt a pale blue. As impossible as it seems, the room became colder. I began to shiver and struggled to prevent my teeth from chattering. Several in attendance stood in unison and began to back away from the fireplace. Panicked eyes first regarded the blue flames and then turned their attention my way. One of the patrons pointed towards me.

"'Tis a sign!" he stammered, overturning his stool as he backed away from the fireplace, a look of terror etched on his face.

"The girl walks once more!" cried another, his features lost in shadow.

"Hush up!" growled another. "Our fear betrays us!"

I turned towards the barkeep. His confrontational demeanour had now been replaced by one of dread. He appeared pallid, apprehensive, and he mumbled something under his breath, his voice hushed, his tone resentful. Not a word, but a name. A name that I had read several times in my case notes.

Mabel.

I rose early the next morning, keen to start my investigation proper. Having found myself cursed with a sceptical mind, which in later years I would learn to count as a blessing, I could not help but wonder whether the preceding night's events had been but a jape at my expense. Indeed, it was not beyond the realms of possibility that the locals, wise to my intentions, had come up with a dastardly plan to either mock or frighten me, in the hope that I might abandon my cause and flee back home to Manchester.

My morning had been spent knocking on the doors of cottages that formed the hub of Alverton. I had received no answer. Though a great many of the villagers laboured in the forest, I knew the wives and children remained at home. I concluded that they must be shy of strangers and sought answers to my questions in the valley below.

As I picked my way through the forest, descending further into the valley, all manner of outlandish theories crossed my mind. I wondered if the blue effect of the flame had been orchestrated by the burning of a mineral I was unfamiliar with. Mother Nature holds many secrets—perhaps such material was abundant in these parts? A simple enough practice it would have been to extinguish the fire while my back was turned, only to add the mysterious fuel and set it alight in the chaos of the darkness. It would have been an easy idea to execute, though the faces of those who had witnessed the spectacle had given naught but the impression of genuine fear. Fear is a look that is difficult to falsify. The faces of the patrons had stricken fear not only in my heart but in those of one another too. Try as I may to rationalise said incidents, I could not satisfactorily explain away their alarm.

Having reached the foot of the valley after a steady and ponderous descent, I concluded that a hoax, possible though it may have been, was unlikely. The air of palpable dread that had descended upon us had not been the result of play-acting or misdirection.

The descent had passed without incident. I was able to find a loggers' path, which guided me safely through the thickest areas of the forest with ease. Voices that at first had sounded sporadic and distant, heard only due to the good fortune of the prevailing wind, now came at me from all sides. The woodland kept their owners hidden from view, but I concluded I was among a large working party that had based themselves beside the banks of the Churnet.

This was a landscape as picturesque as any England had to offer. The river gurgled through the valley base, cutting a twisting path between rock and grass. The sound of the water soothed me, and as the mid-morning sun beat down, any notion that this place harboured a dark and terrible history seemed at that moment improbable.

After a time, I called out. I required the thoughts of the loggers on the rumours that dogged their village. Spending my morning enjoying the scenery would provide few answers. Almost at once, all sounds of work ceased, and a silence settled over the forest, one which tugged me hard from my fancy and left me feeling more than a little unnerved.

Faces began to appear among the trees. Unfriendly faces. Distrustful faces. Angry faces. Not one of them uttered a word; they merely stood half-hidden in the forest and stared. I spoke first and introduced myself.

"Don't matter what yer name is," interrupted one of the faces.

"Nothin''ere of interest for the likes of you," added another.

A mumble of agreement erupted from the treeline.

I asked them if they were able to spare a moment to answer a few questions I had regarding the stories that tarnished the reputation of the area.

"Tall tales they are!" shouted a voice from behind me. I turned to see who had answered only to be met with another set of half-hidden dirtied faces. All remained within the limits of the trees. All eyed me with suspicion.

Unnerved, I continued to press. I explained that people from the surrounding area disappeared around this time of year.

Silence.

I ventured the theory that Alverton and Oak Moor might have an idea as to why that might be.

"Why'd that be then?" answered another.

I turned again. It was impossible to identify who had responded, but I felt I should at least make an attempt to engage whoever might be speaking by facing in what I judged to be his direction. It irked me that none of the loggers would talk to me in the open. I wondered if they were afraid to break ranks? To single themselves out in front of the others as the one who had said too much?

I continued with my theory that the disappearances related to the death of a young woman and explained that she was thought to have been executed for witchcraft in the area, some years before.

Again, nothing but silence.

I dared her name.

Silence again, but of a different sort. I felt a shift in the atmosphere—how best to describe it? Apprehensive perhaps, and tinged with fear.

"Just a story that, nothing more. We don't 'ang folk 'ere."

My heart thumped hard, and my stomach lurched. I'd not mentioned anything of hanging. Whether brave or foolhardy, the words were already said. They lingered, loud and distinct, in the silence that followed. Another shift in the atmosphere now, one loaded with accusation and betrayal.

I heard the gentle snapping of branches erupt and fade into the distance. The faces were gone. I stood and wondered what I was to make of this rebuff. Was it to be interpreted as a sign of collective guilt? Perhaps. Or maybe they had simply grown weary of my attempts to extract an admittance from them. Either way, I stood alone on the riverbank, unsure as to my next step. The villagers and the loggers were reluctant to speak with me, that much was clear, and I had yet to uncover any factual evidence regarding the alleged disappearance. My investigation looked to have met an end.

A voice, one I had not heard during my exchange with the loggers, spoke from behind me. "You want to know about the girl?"

Startled, I turned to see a thin, elderly gentlemen stood before me. His ragged clothes hung from his filthy, slender frame, and heavy shadows lined his bloodshot eyes. I answered that I did. The man nodded and licked his lips. "I'll tell you what they told me as a boy, but it'll cost ya a decent meal."

I reached into my pocket and offered the man a handful of coins.

✣

Aside from the barkeep, myself and the dishevelled old man from the riverbed, the tavern was empty. Since leaving the valley, my dinner guest had said little of note, instead choosing to discuss the possible dishes upon which he may dine.

The scowling barkeep placed a bowl before the old man and retreated into the kitchen. My companion began to hurriedly scoop spoonfuls of stew into his mouth. "'Tis the best stew round 'ere for miles," he mumbled between mouthfuls. "Cecil may be the mean sort, but 'e can't 'alf cook!"

He introduced himself as Thomas and explained that he had worked the forests as a logger for the last thirty years. "Earl's been good to us folk…kept us in work when those further north had nowt," he explained. "Always trees to be felled, always work for those like me!"

Thomas set his empty dish aside and used the tattered remains of his sleeve to wipe his mouth. "Good meal that, but a debt is a debt…you wanna know about the girl, right?"

I straightened in my seat. Having spent the entirety of my time in his company doubting whether he would even approach the subject again, my interest was now piqued. As he smiled at me, I could see shredded strips of meat hanging between his broken yellow teeth. What little appetite I had quickly faltered.

"Yer talk all fancy-like but it won't do yer no good. Not with these round 'ere. I'll tell yer what I know, though yer'll call me a liar, so yer will."

I assured Thomas that I would do no such thing, eager as I was to hear his testimony.

His eyes narrowed, and he searched my face for mocking. Finding none, he continued. "Mabel, she lived in this village nearly 'undred years ago. Quite the beauty by all accounts—some say that was what got 'er into the trouble in the first place. It was said she was a temptress of men—at least, that was one of 'er curses…so they said, the womenfolk at least. Truth be told, she was blamed for every piece of ill luck that fell upon this village. Winters are harsh here, even now. Back then crops failed, food became scarce, and Mabel, with 'er bewitchin' looks and devil tongue, she made no friends in it all. They came to see 'er as a witch. I see yer raise your eyebrow at that, but it was all too common a thing back then. I know. I read."

I nodded and urged him to continue.

"Then there was the missing child. 'Appened right in the middle of the worst times for crops. Someone said that Mabel were to blame for the child turning up dead in the river…" He paused, letting the revelation hang in the air.

I asked whether he believed Mabel was to blame.

"Story goes that she never said either way, so I dunno. Aye, she stood trial an' all but never spoke in her defence."

I asked whether there was any truth to stories of her execution.

"Aye, carried out below…at the old oak. I can show yer?"

My resolve strengthened at his willingness to cooperate; I asked if he would take me to the place of her death.

"Aye, I can…if you have the stomach for it. I'll warn yer now, though, this ain't like any oak you ever saw in your city, boy!"

Fascinated and confounded, I questioned him further.

"'Tis the oldest tree in the valley, probably the land…so far as round 'ere anyways. She holds the earth between strong fingers, thick as you and me. Alas, this is not all."

Captivated by his description of the oak and confident that it was the Wytching Tree he described, I leaned closer.

"When they 'ung 'er, it didn't go to plan. The branch she dangled on snapped. She fell to earth, smashed her legs up good. It was then she cursed us. She said we'd pay for our ignorance, or summat like that, unless the day of her suffering were marked with death."

For a moment, neither of us uttered a sound as I allowed his words to settle into my thoughts.

"But the oak, oh woe…'tis like no other. If a tree could display torment, then this would be it, like something out of the dark forest which Dante traversed as he descended to Hell it is…"

"Tom." It was the voice of the publican, measured and even.

"Oh, I'll take yer," Thomas continued, his eyes wild with danger. "I'll take yer now, but I know she'll be near, she always is!"

"Tom!" barked the barkeep again. Thomas motioned me to lean in closer. "'Tis not safe to talk here," he whispered. "Come see me shortly. My cottage is at the top of the road, second on the right. I'll tell yer more there." He stood quickly, knocking the table as he did so, nodded to the publican and hurried out of the tavern.

I allowed his words to settle while I finished my meal under the watchful glare of the barkeep. It was true that Thomas was a curious fellow: one might even think him eccentric. But a liar I believed him not to be. The story had struck a chord within me. The conviction etched upon his face spoke louder than any words he had used to tell his tale. Thomas believed the stories he had told me, of that I was certain.

I ate, and I wondered what could be so unique about the oak of which he spoke. I wondered if they did hang Mabel Othan all those years ago. I wondered about the curse and its connection to the reported disappearances.

"I'd pay no heed to the talk of that one," said the publican, interrupting my thoughts. "A bit wrong in the head, if you know what I mean."

My own head full of questions, I paid the landlord, bid him farewell and made my way towards Thomas's cottage.

❖

It was approaching dusk by the time I left the tavern, yet nary a soul stirred in the village. I located the cottage which Thomas had claimed as his home and was about to announce my arrival with a firm knock when I realised the door was slightly ajar. Tentative, I pushed it open and took a step inside.

The cottage's sparse interior appeared to be in disarray. Crude wooden furniture lay overturned and broken, half-covered by faded, hole-speckled blankets. It was dark inside, and my eyes took a moment to adjust to the gloom. All was deathly still.

I called out, my voice faltering, betraying my aura of calm. There was no response. I picked my way through the debris, mindful that I did not cause further damage. It was evident that Thomas was a man with few possessions. I wished not to add to his hardship.

Towards the back of the room was a small doorway, absent a door. The ceiling was low here, and I ducked through the opening into what appeared to be Thomas's sleeping quarters. I felt my stomach lurch as my eyes fell upon him. He lay facing upwards across his bed. His eyes stared unblinking towards the ceiling. His mouth hung open, and his tongue lolled to one side. His throat was cut from ear to ear: the thin mattress beneath him was sodden with blood.

I retreated from the scene, my mind a whirl. Nausea took hold of me, and I staggered towards the open doorway, desperate for air. I had not set eyes upon the dead before this day, and the shock of such a sight left me feeling dizzy and sick. In my haste, I did not see them approach me from the shadows, though they must have come at me from either side. I remember that I was struck about the head. Light flashed somewhere behind my eyes. It was a curious experience, one devoid of sound or feeling. What followed was infinite black.

The cold slap of water on the flesh of my face roused me from unconsciousness. As my senses untangled themselves, I realised my precarious predicament. It was night and I was in the forest. Rough hands beneath my armpits supported my weight, though I was now able to do so myself. I was atop a long flight of worn stone steps. Gathered far below was a sizeable crowd. I deduced that the majority of the village were in attendance, and judging by the size of some, the children too—though I could not say who was there, for all gathered wore crude sack masks. Some carried torches. The flicker of the flames threw macabre shadows which danced across the stitched faces, reminding me of the jack-o'-lanterns which illuminate All Hallows' Eve. The itch and pinch which constricted my throat meant it was likely I was wearing a noose. I managed to turn my head slightly to the left, where I saw four hooded men holding the other end of the rope, which I assumed was thrown over an unseen branch high above me. The noose tightened at their every movement, no matter how subtle. I admit now that panic spread through me, and I began to struggle against the grip of my captors.

The crowd, amused by my fear, started to bay and jeer until one among them commanded silence. A tall figure emerged from within their throng and began to take measured strides towards me. Though the figure wore a sackcloth mask, I could feel his eyes upon me. There followed nothing but the sound of my panicked breathing and the slow, deliberate footsteps upon stone.

With barely a foot between us, the figure in the sack mask spoke. "You come here, asking questions, judging us, our way of life, which you know nothing about." It was expressed as an accusation rather than a question.

I was not sure whether an answer was required, so I opted to remain silent. Thoughts of escape ran through my mind, but I had no plan as to how I might accomplish such a feat. I was caught in a hopeless situation, miles from home, miles from help. At that moment, I believed this was to be my end.

"You say nothing?" continued the masked figure, a note of impatience in his tone. Well spoken, I assumed he was either not from the area or of a higher social standing. "These are dark times for us, and measures are in place to assure that we see the light again."

The crowd remained silent and still, poised for the inevitable, practiced in their wait.

"You fail to grasp that which is your fate!" said the masked figure, leaning close to me. I could smell the wine on his breath, rich and fruity. He turned to face the crowd below, throwing his arms into the air. "The day has come! She shall have her sacrifice! We shall prevail for another year—for this, we give thanks!"

The crowd murmured in response and the forest fell silent again. The masked figure turned towards me and whispered, "This is our gift."

At that moment, the four men holding the rope pulled in unison, and I felt an intense pressure around my throat. My feet were free of the ground. Instinctively I started to kick and struggle. This intensified the ferocity of the pressure around my throat. As they pulled, my body jerked and the rope gripped tighter. The crowd roared, barely audible now above the thunderous rush of blood which flooded my ears. I hung, pathetic and helpless, swinging in a wide arc due to the momentum generated by my futile struggles. I knew that death was imminent.

At first, I thought that my eyes deceived me. Starved of oxygen, the mind can conjure all manner of illusions, and I'll wager that it is many a man whose last glimpse of life is one of hope. Before me, from left to right, the flames of the torches carried by the crowd flickered from orange to blue. Again, I cannot be sure of the events that followed, for consciousness came and left in rapid, unpredictable waves, but whatever transpired was enough to save my life.

The crowd began to panic. Torches were dropped and the mob, suddenly fearful, dispersed into the depths of the forest. The masked man who had ordered my execution remained, shouting orders, trying to regain calm. With one last effort (and perhaps my dying breath), I looked to the left and watched through blurred eyes as the men who had hoisted me from my feet let go of the rope and fled into the darkness.

I crashed to the ground, numb and barely alive. Though I broke my arm in several places, I felt no pain at the time. My last memories of that night are of lying in the dirt atop those stone steps. The masked figure was somewhere nearby, shouting frantically into the darkness. His commands went unheeded.

I do recall observing a figure approach the masked man from behind, though one cannot wholly rely on the accuracy of memories formed in a state near death. A young woman with black hair almost to her waist emerged from between the scattered blue flames. She wore a tattered cream dress that seemed to shine with a faint blue aura. She placed her hand on the back of the masked figure, who stood screaming commands, oblivious to her presence. Upon receiving her touch, he fell to the ground.

Quiet returned to the woods, and I lay back, weak and helpless, no longer caring as to my fate. From the mud, I saw that the branches above me were lashed with heavy chains, and though I attempted to fathom why, a now-familiar darkness swallowed me once more.

One

THE MAN I WAS

My visit to the Wytching Tree afforded me an education outside what one might ordinarily expect when visiting a quaint English village. I did not return to that place, but I did inform the constabulary of the murder of Thomas. However, I made no mention of the attempt on my own life. I wished to draw no attention to myself. I had no idea how far the reach of the village might extend. A mistake, perhaps? I ponder upon my decision often. I learned later that arrests were made, and the kidnappings ceased, though this occurred in 1873—two years after my visit. Could I have halted their malicious practice sooner if I had mentioned my brush with death? It is entirely possible that I could, though fear of reprisals, fear of being ridiculed and mocked, my character being marked as questionable before I had even begun to establish myself as an investigator of peculiar tales, all conspired against me. I doubted myself. I doubted my memories, but most of all I questioned my understanding of what had occurred in Alverton. I was weak.

There, already an admission that has taken me by surprise. I am sure there will be more to follow. Writing this, I feel a burden lifted. Yes, I was weak. I was afraid to admit that I had attempted to solve a case involving kidnapping, witchcraft and murder single-handedly. I was scared to admit that I had failed at my first attempt at an investigation. My fear of failure would need to be overcome. It would trouble me often, but that was neither the time nor the place to confront it. So I buried the memories of the Wytching Tree, intending to face my concerns later in life, when I felt better equipped, when I felt better able to understand.

So often do we tell ourselves *later*, finding comfort in our refusal to face our fears. Said comfort is fleeting, for those fears that are buried are only ever temporarily out of mind. I pressed on with my work (as you shall read) with a newfound vigour, born of my failings regarding the Wytching Tree. I reassured myself time and again that the work I undertook meant that I could make a difference to the lives of others, that I could atone for my cowardice. It was a mistake not to speak out and tell the whole story, I know that now, admit that now. The simple truth is that I approached the community of Alverton with the aim of unearthing the truth of their crimes before I was mentally prepared to do so. There were forces at work that I could not hope to comprehend, not at such a young age. Not when I understood so little of the ways of the world.

There is no excuse for cowardice. Though the foul practice that occurred in that community was halted, I could have halted it sooner. At least one life was lost that I might have been able to save.

After a month of restful mental rehabilitation, determined to make amends, I turned my attention towards a fresh investigation. One not concerned with death or witchcraft, one that I convinced myself I would be able to carry out successfully.

Forgive my fervour; often I am caught in a trail of thought and find myself becoming quite carried away. Let us start at the beginning, returning to a time before I ventured into that cursed valley, to a time when I still believed that the answers to the mysteries of life—though well hidden—were waiting to be uncovered, waiting to be understood.

Looking in the mirror of late, I scarcely recognise the withered face that stares back at me. It is June 1914, and global tensions run high. Perhaps impending war is the catalyst to these memoirs, or perhaps it is simply the march of time and the recognition of my declining health which have pressed me into documenting my life's work.

My name, should it matter, is Solomon Whyte. I was born into a family of wealth and standing, one of Manchester's most prominent. For all intents and purposes, it seemed that my destiny was set and I would follow in my father's footsteps in the textile business. Thus, I was educated on the nuances of the industry from an early age. It was often joked that I had cotton in my blood, though this reduced me to tears countless times as a young child. I feared that my body would cease to function at any moment, my veins clogged with an abundance of thread—such is the imagination of the young. Perhaps it was this initial fear that shaped my dislike for the mills?

My father was a good man, wise and staunch. He employed many from the city and was revered among the poor as kind and sincere. The truth, as ever, was not always so pleasant. The adage 'you must be cruel to be kind' was never so true as it was in the factories. Father worked his employees hard. Long hours and meagre pay meant that production maintained a steady pace and Father was able to compete with nearby mills while still turning a profit. Alas, with the invention of the flying shuttle, fewer workers were needed, and he found himself tasked with returning a great many of them to the same streets he had previously plucked them from.

This was a difficult period for the family business, and in a matter of weeks, our name had gone from revered to loathed. I decided soon after that I would not be following in my father's footsteps after all.

My mother was a homely, quiet woman. Having never wanted for anything, she became withdrawn from the world and hardly ever left the house. I remember few conversations with her, as more often than not her words were trite or cutting. Her bitterness, I later learned, was born of long years of solitude. She was a lonely woman, who at one time had hoped to travel the land and immerse herself in the history of this great isle. When I told her of my intended path, I expected a harsh scolding. I believed I would be seen as dishonouring the family name by not continuing in my father's business. Instead, she smiled at me, took me by the hand and said nothing. A solitary tear landed upon her skirts, yet it was me from whom it fell.

A quick aside is in order regarding the origins of my passion for history. I was schooled at the University of London, and though my studies centred upon the topic of business (as my father intended), I quickly fell into a friendship with lecturer of history Dr Geoffrey Osbourne.

Dr Osbourne was a colourful character of staunch belief and tempestuous nature. He taught me that history was not the mere listing of historical events, but the study of the politics and social climate which befell the areas of said events, before, during and after. History is as much a study of people and attitudes as it is names and dates. Long were the discussions we held, sometimes until the small hours of the night, and fascinating were their outcomes. It was here that my interest in folklore began.

Folklore, like history, is passed from generation to generation. Is spoken of over ale and meat, is recounted from parent to child. Like history, its stories contain warnings or advice that are better heeded than ignored. Like history, there is always a substantial truth buried at its heart, no matter how colourful or outlandish the tale. For example, Arthur Pendragon, better known as King Arthur, features prominently in English folklore, though there are historical truths contained within many of the stories pertaining to his exploits. Here, then, folklore and history are intrinsically linked, and the separation of fact from fiction becomes almost impossible. Almost.

In the beginning, I did not believe any of the tales I set about investigating, at least not at first. Some might argue that I have wasted away the days of my life. I shall claim that I have not. The purpose of these recollections is to explain my journey, if not to your interest or understanding, then perhaps for my own. Perhaps documenting my experiences will enable me to pinpoint exactly which decisions shaped which parts of my character. Perhaps. Reflection of this magnitude is a first for me; indeed, many of the stories I am about to relate I have spoken of only to a trusted few.

I can say with a great degree of certainty that once I had settled on my chosen path, the world I imagined as a young man soon ceased to exist, and in its place, I found one of darkness and menace, the likes of which only the cursed few are privy to.

Do I regret the choices I made? Perhaps some, though I will wager that they will not be the choices you might expect. Regret is a vital part of life, a necessary process. It allows us to quantify our standing, enables us to reflect, and if we so desire, to improve. You, dear reader, carry regret—of that I have no doubt. It is only the ignorant who are truly free of it.

Permit me to wander from topic for a moment, as I am caught in the grip of a powerful memory from my childhood that I feel is only fitting to share. Forgive me, memories clamour for my attention in no particular order and I feel that if I do not share them right away, they may fade and not resurface for quite a time.

I would have been eight, and though I am walking along a narrow lane, I am at a loss as to where this memory may have taken place. I am alone save for the family dog, Horatio. The recollection of that name brings a smile to my face, for I had heard no other name so regal sounding as that as a boy. He was an obedient dog, a spaniel, pure of breed. It was assumed that he passed away one winter, for he ventured into the forest behind our home one morning and was not to return. I remember feeling distinctly heartbroken upon his loss. That was the first time I experienced grief, though it certainly would not be the last.

I digress. Back to the lane. It is noon. Horatio is ahead of me and has veered sharply to the right. I jog in a half-hearted attempt to catch up. I hear him bark and see him run beyond the hedgerow. I panic, feeling suddenly anxious at being so far from my dog, and quicken my pace. The fog is thick. It suffocates me, forcing its way into my lungs, prompting me to cough and wheeze. It presses upon my skin with its cold, wet touch. I reach the stile where Horatio entered the field and I climb over it, cursing the dog.

There is nothing before me but a wall of grey. Visibility is but a few feet in either direction. I step forwards, and the stile behind me disappears into the murk. Horatio's barks come quicker now, and to my ears, he sounds under stress. I push forth into the gloom using nought but my ears for guidance.

There is a squeal of pain far ahead of me as Horatio begins to yelp and whine. I know that he is hurt.

I run.

I run until my lungs burn.

I run until my ears sting and my eyes pour, yet I am no nearer to my beloved dog. His cries seem distant and broken. I realise that I have no idea in which direction my injured dog lies. I concede that I am lost.

The fog surrounds me. It invades me, becomes part of me. I feel the chill of its touch coursing through my veins. In my mind's eye, my blood has turned from red to blue. My head screams in pain, my heart thunders in my chest. Sight and sound soften. My senses are numbed, rendered useless by the prevailing gloom. I could lie down and sleep now were it not for the cold. The urge to do so is almost overpowering, but I resist. To me, this feels like the very fringe of death.

A strained whine from somewhere far away.

Overcome with panic, I whirl and spin in a vain attempt to locate the direction of Horatio's cry. It is then that I see her. Far to my left, a shadow, short, and slender. I see her hair, which is long, almost to her waist. She stands motionless, a beacon of life in this field of limbo. She is wearing white. It is a plain dress. I feel no threat and move towards her.

With each step I take, the figure moves away. I hasten my pace and she does likewise. Regardless of my speed, I close no distance.

Meanwhile, Horatio's cries are becoming louder and more distinct. The figure is leading me towards my injured pet, of this I am sure, and I break into a sprint.

Horatio lies before me, his back leg twisted and broken. Pain and fear dull his eyes. I lift him into my arms, elated to have found my dog, then unsure as to my next action. I look around, hoping to source a way out of this place. Again I catch the outline of a figure, short and slender, dressed in white, barely visible through the gloom. I walk towards her, cradling my dog. The shape of the girl disappears, to be replaced by that of the stile.

❖

Horatio's leg mended in time, and my youthful mind chose not to dwell upon the mysterious figure in the fog-shrouded field, at least not until just now. Though I can never be sure, perhaps this was my first encounter with a spectre. I can say that I felt no fear in the presence of said individual, but her manner and her actions were certainly out of the ordinary. For instance, why did she not call to me at any point? Why did she not aid me further and help with the carrying of my dog? Then it must be asked where on earth she vanished to. Though my eyes were young, I recall clearly that she melted away, only to be replaced with the outline of my means of escape. Perhaps she was a deceased relative? Or a fellow lover of animals who was not content to sit by and watch my feeble attempt at rescue?

Many times I wondered whether I had slipped into an alternate plane of existence, so disconnected from the rest of the world felt

I. Reality lay but several hundred yards from me, yet I could sense little in the way of nearby substance while lost in the fog that day.

Though I knew it not then, this was to be the beginning of many journeys into the peculiar, journeys that are recorded here not only for future reference but for means of personal analysis. I hope to find the process of documenting my memoirs therapeutic. I have demons to exorcise and fears to face that I have kept hidden away in the darkest recesses of my mind for far too long. Many times I have doubted my sanity, as have others, and I am certain you will too. What I commit to the following pages is the truth, or at the very least it is my truth. The truth experienced by me, felt by me, feared by me.

Two

THE DRESSMAKER'S MANNEQUIN

Manchester, May 1871

Having decided that I would pursue my interest in folklore and tales of the curious, I opted to investigate a claim originating close to the family home. Perusing the *Manchester Standard* one morning, I came across an article discussing the unusual behaviour of a dressmaker's mannequin. The shop, located in Eccles, had recently acquired a new model, which had been shipped in from Peru. The owner of the mannequin, Lady Dunmore, stated that she had obtained the dummy to add a sense of vigour to her tired window displays. What followed was a series of unexpected events that eventually led her to summon the local priest. The mannequin, it was claimed, came to life at night.

Eccles was but a short walk from my residence, so one summer morning, I set off to visit the shop for myself, keen to speak with Lady Dunmore and with the intention of offering my services. I wagered that this could not be as harrowing an investigation as my last at the Wytching Tree, and felt that this would be the ideal case in which to reacquaint myself with the world of the peculiar.

Elegance Dressmaking Services occupied the last building of a long line of trade premises. Lady Dunmore informed me that it was quite the rarity to find women involved in matters of industry and that she had battled resistance from the moment she had opened her shop. The tiny premises, located far from the busy high street, afforded only a sliver of space. This was the only premises the landlord was willing to let to a female, and Lady Dunmore, ever the resourceful type, made do the best she could.

Against all odds, custom was high amongst ladies of leisure, who—once hearing of Lady Dunmore's endeavours—seemed only too eager to visit her premises and purchase her wares.

Though crooked and crumbling on the outside, inside the shop was immaculate and well presented. There was a large selection of dresses and other attire hanging on racks to the left side of the store, with fitting rooms to the rear. A large, ornate mirror and a clear area of floor occupied the space to the right.

The mannequin took pride of place in the shop's only window. On my visit, it was attired in a trim, floral-patterned silk piece, which Lady Dunmore informed me was inspired by the styles of the Japanese. She explained how her increasing boredom had led her to learn the art of dressmaking, her talent for which had carried her into the beginnings of a business. She remarked that she had met fierce competition from her male counterparts and had at first believed that a hoax was in effect with regard to the actions of the mannequin, the desired outcome being that she cease trading out of fright.

Never the sort to wilt in the face of adversity, she had turned the situation to her favour by electing to inform the local newspaper. Visitors to her shop increased, as did her trade. She argued that if she were the subject of a hoax, all activity would have ceased when the perpetrators saw their efforts had had the opposite effect to their intentions. Suffice to say the mannequin continued her twilight movements.

Having closed the shop early so that I might study the mannequin, Lady Dunmore proceeded to outline the events that had blighted her shop since the arrival of the model. The figure had arrived several weeks earlier, on a trade ship named the *Elsa Maye* that had travelled from South America carrying an assortment of cargo. Lady Dunmore had been in the city of Liverpool the day the ship had come in and had happened to notice the mannequin sitting amongst an assortment of goods on the side of the dock. She explained to me how she was immediately taken by the appearance of the model, citing that it appeared most lifelike, especially in the eyes. A deal was struck with the ship's captain, and the mannequin returned to the shop with Lady Dunmore.

Having spent several minutes examining the model, I could certainly see why she was so struck with its appearance. Mannequins tend to be composed of wicker and to resemble only a very crude human form. This particular model resembled a young woman. She would have been no older than twenty and was strikingly detailed; one might even have called her beautiful. She seemed to be constructed entirely of an unidentifiable resin, which gave her skin a yellow tint. Further, the mannequin had hair that felt human to the touch. Similarly, it had both finger and toenails. Lady Dunmore insisted that her mouth contained a full set of teeth. I asked how she knew this to be the case when the mouth of the mannequin was sealed shut. She explained that depending on the mannequin's movements in the night, this was not always the case.

After obtaining permission, I examined the figure of the mannequin in closer detail. I must admit that I felt at odds with myself removing items of clothing to peek at the body contained within when the subject appeared so lifelike. My mind seemed to delight in my unease and at one point conjured up the illusion of a playful giggle escaping the closed mouth of the mannequin.

I explained to Lady Dunmore that movement would be quite impossible as I could find no hint of a seam or joint which would allow a change of posture. I offered the theory that perhaps she had imagined a slight change of stance or that any impression of movement might possibly be caused by an optical illusion. I argued that dressing the mannequin in various outfits, all of which would sit differently on her form, perhaps catching the light at peculiar angles, might give the impression of a change of pose. She merely smiled and offered that I spend the night in the store and see for myself.

Feeling nothing to fear, I accepted her challenge. The shop held little in the way of a hostile atmosphere; in fact, it was pleasantly warm and extremely well furnished. Having vowed to Lady Dunbar that I would approach the forthcoming evening from a scientific angle, I made a quick visit to the factory stores to procure a quantity of powder most oft used to help lubricate some of the larger machines. Again after seeking permission, I proceeded to scatter the powder onto the floor at the base of the mannequin. Beginning at her feet, I circled the model, moving a short distance further from her with each revolution. I explained to Lady Dunmore that this would help rule out physical manipulation of the model, in that should there appear footprints or scuffs in the powder and the mannequin have changed position, then we could be sure that somebody had approached her during the night. Before Lady Dunmore's departure, I wrote a brief description of the mannequin's clothes and posture, which both Lady Dunmore and I verified to be true before signing. The report read thus:

'At the hour of closing on 5th May, the mannequin at the source of the alleged activity is wearing a silk, floral dress (with a turquoise base). She looks out upon the street to the left. Her left arm is folded across her midriff and her right hand rests upon her right thigh. This I deem to be an accurate and appropriate description.'

Having thanked Lady Dunmore for her time and hospitable offer, I bid her good evening and settled myself for what I assumed ought to be a restful night.

✤

I dreamt of her—the mannequin, I mean. I saw her imbued with life. We were together in a crowded market. It was hot here, and the skies were blue. The people here were dark-haired and olive-skinned. In the distance, I could hear jovial music, and I could taste salt on my lips. The soft cry of a gull floated on the warm breeze. This was not Manchester, nor any other place I had visited, yet it appeared to me so vividly. Wherever this place was, at that moment I numbered among its people. The mannequin girl led me by the hand through the clamour of the marketplace. I had to run to keep up with her as she skipped and darted through the crowds. I'd ask her name, and she would look at me and laugh, urging me to follow.

We entered a large, sand-coloured building where many men lay about smoking from tall, silver ornaments, played games with wooden chips or argued loudly in a tongue foreign to my ear. Still, she urged me forwards, almost wrenching my arm from its socket, through many rooms and past innumerable confused spectators.

Finally, exhausted, we emerged into a great hall. The dance floor was filled with couples arm in arm, moving to a piece of music that was beautiful to my ear, but one I could not name. The girl and I were stood in the centre of the floor when the music suddenly stopped. Each of the couples ceased their dance and turned their attentions to us. An expectant silence followed, and I looked to the mysterious girl for a hint as to what I should do. Her hand reached towards me, and I accepted it in mine. She smiled at me, and my soul felt light and giddy. The band began to strike the first note of the next dance and—

✤

I awoke with a start, the shop unnaturally cold and my breath twisted and contorted before me. The weak light of the gaslight situated on the street before the window front cast tall shadows across the back wall. The mannequin's stood the largest of all, and with the flicker of the light, it seemed to judder and dance in a succession of quick, angular movements.

I stood, shaking the dregs of slumber from my head. The cold gnawed at my fingers, and I reached for a thick fur coat I had seen hanging on one of the rails towards the back of the store. With no regard to my vanity, I threw the coat over my shoulders in a bid to drive the chill from my veins. As of yet I had not dared to look upon the mannequin.

The last traces of heightened emotion that I had felt while I dreamt remained, and though they were feelings of a free and playful nature, I knew that here, in the waking world, they were grossly misplaced. I sat huddled in a corner, awake and rational. I would need to cast eyes upon the mannequin sooner or later, or how could I face Lady Dunmore come the morning? I had expected to find nothing untoward, I had expected to report to her no trace of movement, yet I shall admit here in these notes, in my naivety I had overlooked the possibility that there may have been forces at work within the mannequin that I could not hope to understand.

I braved a look towards the mannequin. My heart, which had those past few moments thundered in my chest, missed a beat. Giddy and nauseous, I saw her. She had turned to face me, her arm outstretched towards me, asking me to dance with her, much as she had appeared in my dream. The powder around her base was undisturbed.

❖

I spent the remaining hours of the night awake. The mannequin had indeed changed position in a way most significant to me. I concluded that as I was present in the shop with the intention to investigate, whatever it was that had attached itself to the model had used this opportunity to try to convey a message to me.

The next morning, I recounted the night's events to Lady Dunmore, who, having listened to my nervous chatter, smiled and assured me that she believed every word. When asked as to what I felt was at work here, I admitted I was at a loss. This being only my second investigation, much of what I experienced was new to me. I had read little on the subject of spirits and their means of communication (for that was what I believed to be residing within the mannequin), but I did assure her that whatever the cause of the activity, she need not show concern. I explained the sense of happiness and freedom I had experienced during my dream. I also admitted my fright at seeing the change in posture, but I reassured her that I didn't believe there was any malice in the figure's actions. Whoever this girl had been in life, she had enjoyed dancing, and though she may well have resided within the constraints of the mannequin, she revelled in the garments and the attention that Lady Dunmore afforded her.

Lady Dunmore seemed content with my explanation and asked that any follow-up reports that were to be written in regard to my findings be forwarded to the local newspaper. I agreed to her wishes.

❖

The mannequin remained in the shop window for many years, until a fire gutted the premises in 1896. The mannequin was the only item to remain intact, untouched by flame. I do not know what became of her once she was removed from the site, though the mannequin girl does occasionally visit my dreams, her hand reaching towards mine, beckoning me to join the dance.

Three

THE BLACK LAKE

Leek, Staffordshire, November 1871

It was during the dying embers of summer that I first received correspondence from a land developer by the name of Leopald Thack. Since my last investigation, at the dressmaker's shop, I had spent many hours locked in my study with an assortment of books with the intention of broadening my knowledge of British history and folklore. The article I had penned regarding the dressmaker's mannequin had afforded me a certain degree of local fame, and my letterbox had been flooded with an array of missives detailing all manner of strange occurrences. Most I believed to be the work of hoaxers, and I paid their pleas little attention. However, the letter sent to me from Mr. Thack alerted my curiosity. I must hasten to add that the promise of a substantial payment upon completion of my investigation convinced me further that now was the time to place my studies aside. After all, one can learn so much more from experience than from books alone.

Mr. Thack wrote that he had been charged with the renovation of Blakemere House and her grounds by Mr Joshua Stranfold, and that part of his remit included the draining of Blakemere Pool. Herein lay the problem. If it suited, Thack would meet with me and further outline the issues at hand in person. He went on to explain that such a delicate and significant matter deserved to be discussed man to man, for he feared that a detailed written account would be all too easily dismissed as a hoax.

I replied stating that I would be interested in meeting, and Thack arrived on my doorstep the following week. Over tea, we discussed at length the issues that had plagued the renovation of Blakemere House before our attentions turned towards the lake. "I must begin by insisting I am not in the slightest bit mad," said Thack, placing his empty cup to one side. "The sea holds many secrets, I believe; far more than we can possibly imagine." He paused, his skin flushed red. "Tell me, sir, have you ever heard of a creature called a mermaid?"

I replied that I had read little on the subject but knew that the creature was a concoction of Greek and Assyrian myth.

Thack nodded in agreement. "I have heard the old tales also. Tales, I thought, were all they were, but…" He paused again, seemingly unsure of his next words. He leaned towards me and lowered his voice. "There is something in the water of that lake. I've not seen it, but I've heard it."

I asked as to what he thought he had heard.

"I'm not going to venture the answer that you think, save to say it was big. Very big."

I suggested Thack could have heard the movement of a large fish, or perhaps that of a duck or goose. To jump to the conclusion that I assumed he was angling towards after the earlier mention of a mermaid seemed ludicrous to me. He was not to be convinced.

"I'll stay with fact, for you shall think me insane. Better you hear the tale from Mr Stranfold himself, should you so choose. However, I will say that there are no fish in Blakemere. The pool is murky with peat and clay, the water thick and black. It is no place in which life may thrive. Indeed, no animal will drink from the pool, not any of the cattle that graze on the moors and no bird above it. This I have seen."

I urged him to continue, fascinated by this revelation. The existence of a body of water which animals feared, if Thack described it truly, was worthy of investigation in itself. Yet I knew there was to be more to this tale.

"Its depth is unfathomable," continued Thack. "My workers, before the…" He paused and took a moment to gather his poise before proceeding. "My workers set about draining the pool. They dug a deep furrow to the south and began to pump the water by hand. Day and night they worked and the level did not alter. Not even by an inch. You must understand, the efforts of their labours would have drained any other pool by at least several feet! They continued to work to no avail until…until the sightings began. They said it was a mermaid." He paused, produced a map from the inside of his jacket and pointed first to the location of Blakemere Pool, then to another nearby. "Here, this is Doxley Pool. Finding natural lakes at this altitude is unusual. Both of these lie fifteen hundred feet above sea level. Some say that a subterranean chamber connects the two, hence the water level in Blakemere refusing to dip despite our efforts. It's one theory. One we cannot disprove, anyway."

I regarded the map for a moment. The lakes were situated in Staffordshire. A knot formed in my gut. Was I ready to return to the county where I had almost lost my life?

"Mr Stranfold has offered to accommodate you for as long as needs be. He will explain the sightings in more detail should you choose to take us up on our offer," said Thack as he folded the map and placed it back inside his jacket. "He is a determined sort, and he will not let superstition bar the way of what he deems progress. His mind is set on clearing his land, and the lake is to go. Whether you believe my words or not is irrelevant. Mr Stranfold and I would like you to thoroughly investigate the area surrounding the lake so that we may continue with our endeavours. We have a frightened workforce who refuse to go anywhere near the lake. We shall not interfere with your methods and shall afford you as long as is deemed necessary. You shall be well compensated for your time."

I told Mr Thack that I would indeed consider the offer and that I would be in touch. The idea of a mythical creature inhabiting an inland lake high up in the remote moorlands of Staffordshire intrigued me, as did the prospect of discovering the origins of the tale. Still, the possibility of a hoax remained high. Could it be that the plans made by Stranfold had irked the locals so much that they had created the story of the mermaid in a bid to persuade him to leave the lake as it was? Could it be that *I* was the target of a hoax? Having made somewhat of a name for myself locally, could this be an elaborate ploy, set up to make me appear foolish? All were possible, but there was something in Thack's tone that told me he believed there to be something in the lake. He presented as a man afraid, afraid and unsure of what he was faced with. If this was a hoax, then Thack was an unwitting accomplice.

The story fascinated me, and I wrote the next morning to confirm my interest. A date to meet was hastily arranged and a carriage was sent. I stepped aboard not having the slightest inclination of what to expect with regard to this particular investigation. Would I be unearthing the threads of fabrication, woven in a bid to dissuade the wishes of an unwelcome landlord, or would I reveal the existence of a creature previously believed to be the subject of myth? Though I remained apprehensive for the bulk of the journey, the knowledge that I would be paid in any eventuality soothed my sense of uncertainty.

❖

I arrived at Blakemere House late into the night. Though the moon appeared hidden by cloud, what little light it offered afforded me a decent view of the property. The entire west wing of the house was missing a roof. Timber long exposed to the elements outlined a skeletal shape, giving an indication as to how the house once had stood. The vast majority of the walls had crumbled, beaten upon by the relentless gales that afflicted the moors. Blakemere House stood in ruin.

Mr Thack met me at the foot of the driveway and escorted me into the inner sanctum of the house. He informed me that only the kitchen, study, master and guest bedrooms were habitable but assured me of a restful night nonetheless.

Stranfold was sat at his desk when I entered the study. He did not rise to meet my hand, merely nodding to a vacant seat situated to his left. I took it, introduced myself and waited.

Neither of us spoke until Thack returned with two bowls of stew, a plate of bread and two tankards of ale. Taking the lead from my host, I began to eat. It was Stranfold who spoke first. "Thack says you don't believe in the mermaid?"

I dabbed my mouth with a handkerchief and explained that it was not so much a case of not accepting the merits of the tale outright—more that I intended to find proof of her existence before offering an opinion on the story.

Stranfold began to laugh. He was an old and portly man. Thin wisps of grey hair streaked his round face. Tiny eyes glistened with tears as he coughed and choked on his bread. "My boy! You shall find your proof! Of that, I am certain!" He placed his bowl of stew onto the lip of his desk and stood. "Come with me," he said, beckoning me to follow. He led me to a large window that looked out onto the moors. Blakemere Pool lay to the right, several hundred yards from the house. The smooth surface of the water glinted in the moonlight, offering an almost mirrorlike surface, one which reflected the night sky in perfect symmetry. "Many times I have stood here and watched her swim," began Stranfold, a hint of nostalgia in his voice. "Of course, she never shows herself fully—I only ever catch the ripples of her movement, or on occasion, the sound of her leaping from the water. She is in there; you shall see."

For a moment, the two of us observed the lake in silence. Not once was its surface disturbed.

Stranfold clapped a quick hand on my back. "Come, eat. Let me tell you the tale of how she came to these parts. Though I do hope that you are of a healthy disposition, for mine is not a happy story to tell."

I assured Stranfold that he need not fear and took my seat beside his desk. He patted his round thighs and smiled. "'Course, I don't expect you to believe a word of it. I didn't when I bought the place. Put it down to superstition—those down there in town don't care for me much. I figured it was a story meant to scare me back up north!"

Stranfold went on to tell me how he had acquired the property at auction the summer before last. It was his wish to restore Blakemere House to its former standing, and he assured me that it had been his intention to invest a significant portion of his fortune into the renovations. "Something about the moors speaks to me," he continued. "Some find it lonely up here, but not I. The view on a summer's day is second to none, you can see the heart of England in all of her glory, and who wouldn't want to see that when they wake? Yes, this was to be a great house, only for that cursed lake and the refusal of folk to work here." He explained that his plans to drain the lake had met with fierce opposition from the nearby village of Leek. Labour had been hard to acquire and renovations had progressed slowly. They had halted altogether several weeks previously.

"I'll tell you what they said to me, those from the town. You can decide yourself whether there is any truth in their words. It was 1752 and the crew of the fishing ship *St George's Peril* cast their nets into the Mediterranean Sea. They were fishing the Straight of Sicily, in the hope of landing one final catch before they returned to Portsmouth. Upon hauling their nets on deck, they discovered something most unusual. Caught in the tangles of a net lay a creature that was half-woman, half-fish. The crew christened her a mermaid. With flowing fair hair that settled upon her slender shoulders in tight curls, and skin of pure white, she was quite the most beautiful thing the crew had ever seen. They elected to keep her on board with the intention of revealing her to an adoring British public upon their return. They all agreed that there was more money to be made by showing off their latest catch than by returning to fish the seas.

"One amongst the crew, a young sailor by the name of Benjamin Gosling, took a particular liking to the creature. He spent many hours in her company, and it was said that the two of them fell in love.

"As the days passed, the mermaid's health began to deteriorate. Little did the crew realise that because they had taken her from the water, she was slowly starting to die. She spoke of her desire to feed to Benjamin, who, blinded by his love for her, agreed to help satiate her hunger.

"One by one, Benjamin led the sailors to the mermaid with the promise that she intended to lie with them, and one by one she feasted upon them, leaving nothing remaining but offal and bone.

"As the crew dwindled and the journey home lengthened, the remaining men, suspicious of the disappearance of their shipmates, refused Benjamin's offer to meet the creature to mate. Their fear of the mermaid was high. With his love in danger of dying, Benjamin was forced to release her from her captured state so that she might continue to feed.

"On the eighteenth of September 1752, *St George's Peril* ran aground near the village of Poulton. Not a soul was found on board alive. It is said that Benjamin carried his love from that wreck and sought out a lake in which the mermaid could dwell undisturbed. He came to this place, Blakemere, atop the moors, far from any place, and laid her into the lake. He promised her that he would return, yet having witnessed her murder and devour his crewmates, he realised that he had brought a monster to the shores of England, and he never went back. Some say that the diet of blood and flesh caused the mermaid to transform into something foul and hideous. Indeed, no sighting of her ever describes her appearance as beautiful, save for those in this story."

Stranfold allowed his words to settle before continuing. "It's like this, Mr Whyte. I need labourers to work on the house, and none will come. They are afraid of the lake and what resides within its waters. I'd managed to round up a few willing to work—not enough, granted, but it was a start. They downed tools when she appeared to them, to warn them of what would happen should they drain her lake. They won't come back. Not until this matter is taken care of. That is where you come in."

I finished my stew in silence, pondering on the intricacies of the tale I had heard. Fanciful though it was, there was the possibility that the story contained some degree of truth. The history of the ship could be traced. Records detailing her voyages would easily be obtainable were there a need, yet I struggled to believe that even a man gripped by love would so willingly lead his shipmates to their deaths.

Stranfold observed me in thought, keen to read any flicker of reaction to his words. After a time, he stood. "I've heard her sing, you know. Quite beautiful. Quite haunting. If you find yourself awake at around the time of one, you may hear her song carry faintly through the gale."

I offered him the idea that it might be the wind he had heard. Often it produces notes which might easily be mistaken for melody or indeed, on rare occasion, song. He merely smiled, shook my hand and wished me a good night's rest.

❖

Morning, and a stiff wind blew across the moors. I found I had to angle myself into it to make progress towards the shores of Blakemere Pool. Sudden gusts threatened to steal my balance and I cursed the elements. Though the views of the English countryside were at times breathtaking, this was a godforsaken and desolate place.

The surface of Blakemere Pool lay before me, still and black. The smell of sulphur pervaded here. I took a handkerchief from my pocket and pressed it to my mouth. Thack stood away from the edge, content to observe from a distance. I sank to my knees and trailed my hand through the water. The ripples caused by my movements spread quickly across the pool.

"Cold, ain't it?" offered Thack. I nodded and returned a glove to my hand. "Water's no good for drinking, like I said…full of peat and clay deposits…and more."

I turned and nodded in agreement. Thack handed me the large net that he had carried from the house. "You'll be needing this too," said Thack as he turned and began to make his way back towards the house. "Reckon you'll know what to do come the time."

❖

My initial circumnavigation of the pool revealed little of interest. Around, I estimated it to measure approximately 1,200 feet. In diameter, eighty feet at its widest point. I located the ditch that had been dug to drain the pool, concluding that it was a little shallow for purpose. However, the depth of the ditch would not have halted the process of lowering the level of the lake. Not if the workers had spent as many hours labouring as I had been informed. Was it possible that this lake was connected to Doxley Pool via an underground passage? I turned towards the horizon to my right and shielded my eyes against the glare of the low autumn sun. The other lake was barely visible, but I could not in all confidence rule out such a theory. I knew little of nature and her ways, so I could not rule out the possibility.

I found no evidence of the presence of a mermaid, though I will admit to not knowing exactly what I should look for. There was no activity at all to be noted in or around the area of the pond. What birds I did observe stayed clear of both the lake and me.

❖

Night fell upon the moors and with it a further chill. I was to remain lakeside for the duration of the evening in the hope that I may catch the movement of something within the waters. Under the glare of the moon, Blakemere resembled a vast pool of blood, still and black. The hours rolled by and I began to numb in body and mind as the cold of the night seeped into my core.

❖

I had slept. For how long I was unsure, yet I woke with a start. The wind had ceased at that very same instant, I swear it, and an eerie calm settled over the lake. Faintly—almost unrecognisable at first, so softly did it come—I began to make out the sounds of a harmony, though what produced her notes I could not say. It was most unlike any instrument I had ever heard previously, more akin to the sound a cricket makes when attracting a mate, yet this was not one fixed note but many announcing together in a succession of various timings. This was music! The resultant symphony carried my mind to a far-off place, and momentarily I left the moors and their desolation far behind.

The sound of water being disturbed brought me back to my senses. With the ethereal melody suddenly lost in the fog of my mind, my eyes fixed on the ripples that had emanated from the centre of the pond. I climbed to my feet with the net in hand. My heart pounded, for I was as sure as Thack that nothing could reside within these troubled waters. The sound of movement came again, nearer to shore, nearer to me.

The creature broke the surface of the water not ten yards from my position. It rose to a height of three feet, its yellow eyes glinting in the moonlight. This was not a creature of beauty. Her hair (for I determined it to be female) hung in thick tangles of black. Her face was drawn and skeletal, her nose pinched and pointed. Her flesh emitted a green tinge that gave the creature a glowing aura. She smiled and revealed a mouth lined with many needle-like teeth.

For a moment, we each regarded the other.

Silently she began to glide towards me, the waters parting in her wake. Frozen by fear, I allowed her to reach the shore. She was now within mere feet of me. With a smooth motion, I brought the net down upon her and attempted to pin her to the ground. She began to thrash and struggle to break free. I must confess I had absolutely no idea what I was going to do with the mermaid now that she was within my control, other than hang on until morning and the hope of further help! She managed to back into the water—the power of the creature was remarkable. I was dragged helplessly towards the water's edge until she dived below the surface. I allowed the net to travel with her, but she began to push harder against my grasp. I elected to drag her back to the surface, where I had concluded she was slightly more manageable, but I struggled to do so. As she broke water, the creature uttered a shrill shriek that threatened to pierce my eardrums, and instinct forced my hands to my ears. The net fell to the ground, and the mermaid swam free.

I sank to my knees and examined my hands. They had come away from my ears bloody. I could hear the sound of my heartbeat and little else. Somewhere out of sight, I heard the mermaid break the surface of the water again, followed by a playful giggle.

The rest of my vigil passed without incident.

✣

Thack and Stranfold were only too eager to hear my tale. I delivered a clear description of the creature and recounted my struggle. I advised that in my opinion it would be difficult to try to remove the mermaid from the pool, possibly even dangerous. I had experienced her might firsthand and warned that if her origin story were true, it may well be better to leave her be.

Stranfold seemed amused at my story. In his eyes, I had come to him as the doubter, the fool in the room. I allowed him his moment of satisfaction; after all, it is not often that a story so outlandish is proven true. I bid them both well in the hope that my advice was to be followed. Blakemere was home to a creature no longer of myth, but fact. Excited by this prospect though we were, we decided between us that the Blakemere Mermaid would be better left undisturbed.

✣

When I came to compile this book, I attempted to make contact with Stranfold to enquire as to the well-being of his aquatic guest. I received no reply. Contacting Thack, I was later informed that Stranfold had been found floating in Blakemere Pool some several years previous. It is said that his body was marked with deep lacerations and that his eyes were plucked from his head.

Blakemere House was left to ruin. Today only the lake and its guest remain. I often wonder what possessed Stranfold to seek her out; perhaps it was her song that beckoned him to his death. Alas, I shall never know for sure.

Four

THE INTERNMENT OF THE SAFE

The road to Dartmoor, 1876

Recalling the account of the Blakemere mermaid has stirred another memory, though this incident occurred several years later. I warned that this may well be the case, but please forgive me. I wish to recount this particular tale while it is fresh in my mind.

The year was 1876. I was now held in a position of high regard in terms of my research. I had five years' experience working within the realms of the paranormal (such was the all-encompassing term coined to describe the nature of my work), and I had proven almost as many cases to be hoaxes as to be true. It was the height of summer when I was called to Devon (specifically Dartmoor), with regard to a tale that I shall touch upon in due course.

As was customary, a coach was sent so that I may be afforded the luxury of direct travel. However, it was necessary for the driver to collect several fares along my journey, for though my road was long and the pay good, this was a man with many mouths to feed, and it made perfect sense to collect passengers along the route who could further add to his purse. I minded little. As I had become accustomed to my work, I had realised the importance of observing witnesses during their testimonies. A great deal of truth can be learned not by listening to what is said, but by observing the language of the body. This interest passed into my leisure time, when I would often find myself watching the actions of those around me. Travelling in the company of strangers allowed me to hone my abilities further.

I recall one such gentleman, for quite the character was he. It was the village of Yarnfield where our paths crossed. Upon the morning of our departure, I was greeted by the sight of my driver and a tall, gangly fellow struggling to load what appeared to be a large item of furniture onto the back of the coach. After much huffing and puffing, with little headway made, the driver called for my assistance. No stranger to lending a hand, I immediately obliged, and between the three of us, we were able to manhandle the load into position. The piece was rectangular in shape, wrapped in several layers of dark material, standing at a height of approximately four feet and weighing more than I would hasten to guess. Indeed, the three of us had struggled to move it!

While lifting the load, it had been apparent that there was something large and cumbersome inside the mysterious object, for each of us had felt the shift of weight as we struggled to manoeuvre the heavily wrapped piece into position. When the driver, breathless and red with exertion, asked as to what we were loading onto his carriage, the tall man elected not to speak.

Once it was safely stowed, it was noted that the extra weight had caused the rear of the wagon to sink; it now sat mere inches from the ground. The driver took the tall fellow aside and remarked that to carry the load as far as Devon, an extra horse would need to be added to share the workload.

The tall man nodded.

The driver continued to explain that our departure would be delayed while alterations were carried out to reinforce the rear of the carriage.

The tall man nodded again.

Bemused, the driver informed him that this would add to the price of his passage. The tall man reached into his pocket and handed the driver a handful of coins.

✤

Later that afternoon we departed Yarnfield to continue our journey south, the bulk of which passed in silence. This bothered me little as I had my notes to occupy my thoughts. I was never much of a conversationalist back in those early days. I preferred to keep my business my own and I found pleasantries hard to pass off convincingly. I need not have worried, as my travelling companion kept his attention focused on the passing scenery.

Whenever there was a sudden bump in the road (of which there were many), I noted that my companion would shift in his seat and his attention would move to his parcel, which was stowed behind his seating on the rear of the coach. With a strained look, it seemed as though he would hold his breath a moment, until, finally satisfied, he would return to a relaxed poise and continue to stare out beyond the window.

There were times too when I thought I heard sounds coming from the parcel on the back of the coach. How best to describe them? Perhaps the sounds of something moving around awkwardly inside. My companion noticed my alarm and eyed me with a nervousness which unsettled me deeply. Recognising his anxiety, I hastily concluded that the sounds were caused by the shifting of cargo due to the conditions of the road, and I continued with my notes. My companion's eyes lingered upon me a moment longer, scrutinising me as I worked, until he returned them to the window once more.

✣

We were to bed in Bristol before continuing on into Dartmoor on the morrow. The exact destination of my travelling companion was a mystery both to myself and to our driver. When pressed, he would mumble to keep heading west and would offer no more.

✣

With much of an audience, the three of us unloaded the coach and carried the mystery item through a crowded tavern, up a small flight of stairs and into the room the tall man would occupy that evening. He muttered not one word of thanks.

Fatigued from our exertions, the driver and I retired to the busy tavern and sat for our evening meal. It was a lively place, frequented by sailors, dockers and soldiers alike. We stayed awhile and listened to the chatter. Experience had shown that taverns often proved to be a fruitful source of myth and folklore.

✣

The hour was late when I ascended the staircase that led to my lodgings at the rear of the tavern. My driver had bid me good night an hour or so earlier, and I had elected to remain behind to see if any of the assorted drinkers had heard the tale which I was travelling to investigate. Neither of us had seen any sign of our travelling companion.

As I moved to pass the door to the tall man's room, I paused for a moment. Raised voices could be heard coming from inside, though they were muffled by the closed door. Curious, I pressed my ear to it. I was mistaken. There was only one voice which was raised, a voice I attributed to the tall man. He appeared to be distressed, though I could not fathom why, as I was only able to hear his sombre replies. The voice of the other partaker in this conversation was but a low murmur to me.

There came a sudden scream, and instinctively I pushed the door aside, entering the tall man's room. I meant to aid, not pry, for the scream was one of horror and dread. I saw before me a blur of movement and a tangle of elongated grey limbs, which disappeared into the object that the three of us had struggled to carry to this room, slamming the object's heavy door shut behind it. The tall man and I regarded one another for a moment. "Wh-what did you see?" he asked, his tone uneven, his body shaking.

By light, I could see that the item was a safe, cast in iron. The material in which it had been previously wrapped was folded neatly on the bed. The tall man looked at me, his eyes bloodshot and wide in surprise, likely at my sudden intrusion. After taking a moment to assess the scene, I ventured an answer. I told him that I saw a large safe cast of iron. I told him that I understood now why we had struggled to lift it.

"And?" pressed the tall man, his eyes darting first to the safe and then back to me.

I hesitated, unsure of how to answer.

The tall man sat on the edge of the bed and began to sob. "It is a terrible thing that you saw. Something no man should ever cast eyes upon. It—she—moves, yes, but she is not alive, at least not in any sense that is Christian."

I asked the man to explain further, but he declined. The creature I had momentarily observed had appeared in no way to be human. Short and stocky, with no clear sign of a head, its skin was a grey tone and its arms lolled and trailed behind its torso. I asked if I may open the safe to cast eyes upon the creature again, but the tall man erupted into a rage so unlike his previous nature that I fled the room amidst threats to my safety, should I ever breathe a word to anyone of what had transpired that night.

✥

The next morning the three of us loaded the safe (which was freshly bound and hidden from view again) onto the back of the carriage. The tall man's eyes teased threats of violence, and I chose to devote my attention to my notes. Privately I wondered as to the contents of the safe. What manner of being had I observed the night before? Having interrupted their discussion, I had noted a look of sheer terror on the tall man's face—why was he so afraid of the thing in the safe? These questions and more troubled me, and what had started out as an everyday journey had suddenly become one of serious interest to me and my work.

Again the ride was rough and uncompromising. The sounds of movement continued to emanate from the safe. Though it was never acknowledged aloud, those of us travelling in the carriage knew that not all of the sounds coming from the back were due to the conditions of the road.

✤

It was in a village named Colyton that the tall man instructed the driver to halt; specifically, at the gates of Saint Andrew's parish church. He told us that we must remain stationary until nightfall, and while our driver bemoaned this instruction, having seen the desperate and wild side of the man, I elected to hold my tongue. Our companion reiterated that the driver was to be well compensated for his time, and I was content to observe what might happen after dark. I felt that this journey and indeed this story were fast approaching their conclusion.

✤

The hush of darkness fell upon Colyton. Cottage doors were locked and the winding, cobbled streets emptied of life. Satisfied that all eyes were behind closed doors, the tall man gestured for us to alight. The gates of the cemetery were secured with a chain. The tall man took a long metal pole he had stowed in the back of the carriage and used it to break the links of the chain, allowing us access.

The graveyard was small and well kept. Yet in the blackness of the night, there lurked an oppressive atmosphere. I felt that after dusk, the living, having brought offerings of flowers and paid tearful respects to the deceased, were no longer welcome in this place of rest. The driver and I waited by the side of the carriage, content to leave the tall man to his trespass. He disappeared from sight for several moments before returning to us, a shovel in each hand. "Come," he instructed. "We dig."

Despite our silent protestations, we followed the tall man to an area of the cemetery which afforded us seclusion due to the presence of a large tree. I could see the discord on my driver's face as the three of us set about our task. Though he seemed reluctant in his efforts, I concluded that he was content enough to oblige his passenger's wish given the promise of further payment.

You may ask why I partook in this gruelling effort. Ordinarily I would have forcefully declined such an instruction, opting to stay in the relative comfort of the coach and as far from the muck and exertion that grave-digging entails as possible. As it was, we knew we were digging a grave for something, and though my driver was motivated by coin and had little interest in the *hows* and *whys* of the task, I was driven by that most insistent of emotions—curiosity.

We worked through the bulk of the night. It was not a traditional grave that the tall man ordered us to dig, more a square shaft running to a depth of approximately ten feet. Satisfied with our efforts, the tall man afforded us a short break before ordering us to remove the safe from the back of the carriage.

Again, aside from managing the bulk of the safe, all was well, until we passed through the gates of the cemetery. Were it not for our combined efforts the safe would inevitably have spilled from our hands, such was the force of the sudden movement felt from within. The weight shifted violently from my left to my right, though the three of us managed to catch the tumbling safe with bare inches to spare. The look of horror upon our driver's face as he realised that the item he was carrying contained something *alive* showed pure shock. His hesitation only added to our struggle in keeping the safe aloft.

Breathless, we continued towards the freshly dug shaft. As we drew nearer, the amount of movement coming from inside the safe increased in ferocity, and it was soon accompanied by a muted wail the likes of which no human could muster. This activity continued to intensify with each step taken, testing our resolve.

As we approached the lip of the shaft, the tall man ordered us to set the safe onto the ground. By now the activity coming from inside had reached feverish heights, and I was confident that the shrieks emanating from within would alert those in the cottages neighbouring the cemetery. The tall man urged us to ignore the terrible cries, and together we pushed the safe closer and closer to the edge.

With one final effort, we tumbled the safe into the hole, though it fell at an awkward angle and lodged halfway. Cursing in a foreign tongue, the tall man leapt in and proceeded to jump on it, forcing the safe deeper into the shaft. My driver and I watched in disbelief as the tall man sank further in with every leap until he disappeared from sight entirely.

After a few short moments, he called to us for help, and together we lifted him from the hole. Knowing what must follow, we each took to our shovels and began loading soil back into the earth whence it had come. With each handful of dirt replaced, the screaming and the thrashing emanating from inside the safe diminished, until finally they subsided altogether.

✢

The tall man did not continue his journey west, electing to remain in Colyton to catch a coach heading to London. The driver assured me that he had been well paid for both his silence and his efforts. As for myself, the tall man did offer coin in order that I ask no questions, nor tell of our activities that night, but I politely declined his offer. Though I often wonder what manner of creature we consigned to the hallowed earth that night, I can only assume that the tall man's motives were born of necessity and not desire.

As far as I am aware, she resides there still.

Five

THE SCREAMING SKULL

Burton Agnes, Yorkshire, February 1872

My third investigation (to this day I do not count my time in Alverton as anything other than a failed exercise) came by way of an invite to Burton Agnes Hall. This particular manor house had occupied the same site since the days of the Norman Conquest, changing hands over the centuries not by means of sale but by family lineage. I was instructed to pack for a short stay and informed that I would be briefed as to my duties in person by the lord of the manor. There was little in the way of further information.

Located in Burton Agnes, Yorkshire, the manor house was an impressive example of Norman construction, though I must admit that its subsequent history was of far more interest to me. It seemed that my reputation as an investigator of note had spread further afield than I had dared imagine, having caught the attention of Lord Fawksby, and I was only too eager to begin my work anew.

Upon my arrival, my belongings were taken to my room and I was ushered into the study, whereupon I was introduced to Lord Fawksby. He was a fellow of similar age to myself, and as I listened, I judged him to be well read and of high intellect. We drank excellent port and discussed my previous investigations. Satisfied that there was nothing in his demeanour which would suggest an air of the fantastical, I accepted his invitation to remain as his guest and to investigate the claims of which he spoke at length. Indeed, a crucial part of my investigation focused on the credibility of key witnesses, and this was a skill that I would be able to hone further over the countless cases yet to come.

Presented here, in words told to me by Lord Fawksby himself, is the plight of Burton Agnes Hall.

"You may well know that the hall and its many treasures have passed through the ownership of many generations, yet not one single penny has ever changed hands to procure her ownership. It is blood that inherits the manor, not wealth nor influence, and it is said that many lengths have been taken to keep it so.

"In 1643, the manor and its land were owned by Lady Anna Farlish. History tells us that her husband, Lord Timothy Farlish, was a most unpleasant sort. A letch and a drunk, it is said, he indulged in many extramarital affairs, yet his wife stood resolutely by his side.

"One such affair involved Lady Farlish's sister, Margaret Anstey. She was the younger of the two, and it is said that Lord Farlish had lusted after her for many a year. Margaret fell pregnant by Lord Farlish, who at this time had no immediate heir. With no plans to divorce Anna (for she held the rights to the estate), it is said, he attacked Margaret as she guested in the east wing, stabbing her with a pocket knife in a desperate attempt to rid her of child.

"Sadly, Margaret succumbed to her injuries and died that very night. With her dying breath she cursed Lord Farlish for his deeds, citing that she belonged in the manor house with her family, and should her head not remain perched atop the mantelpiece until the manor did crumble, then each who resided within would suffer terribly.

"The murder of Margaret Anstey was attributed to one of the servant boys and the claim put about that having been spurned in his efforts to woo her, he had attacked her out of fury. He was hanged from a tree in the grounds at the very same time that Margaret was interred in the Anstey family crypt, in Burton Agnes Cemetery, which lay on the opposite side of the village.

"That night, the house was beset by all manner of terrors, so much so that the body of Margaret was ordered exhumed the next morning and her head removed and brought back to the manor."

It was at this point that my host stood and bid me follow him. I asked what specific terror had befallen the house that night, but he did not answer. We left the study and followed a narrow, oak-panelled corridor as it weaved its way through the bowels of the house. After passing several rooms, Lord Fawksby stopped before a set of grand double doors. He searched his pockets for a moment and produced a small key. He paused for breath after turning the key and spoke to me, his eye fixed upon the keyhole. "I shall warn you, no person has set foot in this room in almost a decade. I cannot prepare you for what you may experience in this place. Know that you look upon Margaret of your own will. Yes?"

I nodded and assured him that I wished to continue.

The door eased open with a groan, and we stepped inside. Lord Fawksby threw aside a pair of heavy drapes, thick with dust, and the mid-afternoon sun flooded into the room. I moved deeper inside as my host busied himself with the second set of drapes.

The vast chamber would have served as a dining room at one time; such was its size, shape and location. Though now devoid of all furniture, the air rang with the memories of countless engagements past.

Lord Fawksby began to speak. "There." He pointed, covering his mouth with a handkerchief. "The mantelpiece."

I turned in the direction Lord Fawksby had indicated and saw something sat in the centre of the mantelpiece. With a nod, Lord Fawksby gave permission for me to proceed, and I approached. The object was covered with a black, silken cloth, which despite the environment was utterly devoid of dust. My hand hovered tentatively above it. I knew that beneath this lay the head of Margaret Anstey, and I required a moment to compose myself before unveiling her.

With a quick motion, I removed the silken cloth and stared at the sight before me. The skull was tinged with patches of black and grey. The lower jawbone was cracked and several of her teeth were absent. Though long dead, the gaze of Margaret Anstey seemed to mock my repulsion. I staggered backward, dropping the cloth onto the floor, feeling nauseous and dizzy.

"You are not the first to react so poorly to our permanent guest," remarked Lord Fawksby. "Tell me, do you feel unwell?"

I assured him that whatever sickness had taken upon me had quickly subsided, for several feet away from her, I felt immediately better. I concluded that now was not the time to show distaste, not in front of the man who tasked me with dispelling her myth. I stared at the skull, and the skull stared back.

Lord Fawksby replaced the cloth over the skull, breaking my concentration. "Come, friend," he said. "Let us to your chambers. There shall be plenty of time for you two to become acquainted over the next couple of days."

❖

Much to my surprise, I slept soundly that first night. Any thoughts of the rotted skull of Margaret Anstey remained far from my mind. It was at breakfast I first encountered Lady Jasmine Fawksby. Boiled egg and freshly baked bread in hand, I had seated myself at the foot of the table. Lord Fawksby, having sent his apologies, was conspicuous by his absence, meaning that the table was shared by only Lady Fawksby and me. We engaged in pleasantries and light conversation while the servants busied themselves, and I remember feeling at ease in her company. I guessed her to be a shade younger than myself. She was of similar height and a slender build, and had long, dark hair that lay unnaturally straight. Her face held quite the softest features I had ever set eyes upon and she spoke with intelligence and enthusiasm. Her eyes sparkled with a mischievous nature, and she wielded with ease the sharpest of wit. It would be safe to say that I was enchanted by her presence, and I allowed myself to linger at the breakfast table a while longer than I had initially planned.

She took a keen interest in my ideas regarding the paranormal and revelled in hearing tales of my work. She had several keen theories of her own, though lamented that she had few around her with whom to share her interest. Even her husband forbade her from conducting an investigation into the skull of Margaret Anstey, a practice which I assured her was most unfair. Time slipped quickly by that morning. All too soon was she called away to carry out the duties required of the lady of the manor, and I was left with the lingering feeling that she and I had experienced a unique connection.

✥

It was decided by Lord Fawksby that on the second evening of my stay I would remain alone in the great hall, with nought but the remains of Lady Margaret Anstey, the means to record any observations I might make and a solitary candle. Were it not for the kindness of Lady Fawksby, who in the dead of night sought my company and delivered a thick woollen blanket, I wager that I would have perished, it being so cold! The lady stayed but a few moments, curious as to my findings, before returning to her chambers. What little warmth the blanket afforded seemed to dissipate upon her departure.

Aside from a ferocious wind which seemed to pound the outer walls for the majority of the night, there was little out of the ordinary to note.

✥

I spent a good part of the third day sleeping in the guest quarters, having being granted so little reprieve by the uncompromising weather the night before. I knew that tonight would be where the real crux of my investigative work would begin, for Lord Fawksby had ordered one of the kitchen staff to remove the skull from the mantel and to deposit it somewhere within the gardens. The exact location of Lady Anstey's skull was known only to the lord and the poor wretch ordered to hide her.

✣

It was not long after dusk when the disturbances began. Again I was settled in the great hall, my notes at my side and the thick woollen blanket gifted from Lady Fawksby laid across my lap. At first, the sounds consisted of a series of sharp raps that seemed to emanate from within the area occupied by the fireplace. They would cease whenever I ventured close, so it was impossible for me to identify the exact location of their origin. This game of back and forth continued until approximately one o'clock.

After a brief hiatus, the sound of slamming doors echoed throughout the manor house, followed hastily by heavy footfalls that seemed to walk in several parts of the house at once. Lord Fawksby had instructed that all serving staff remain in their chambers after dark and promised that he and Lady Fawksby would do likewise. Several times did I venture from that room, convinced that I would successfully identify the person whose footsteps at times shook the very fabric of the house. Not once did I observe anyone walking the halls, despite a thorough search. The footfalls continued, gaining in volume. On occasion, they seemed to occur in my immediate vicinity, and to my ears, appeared to be heading straight towards me. Again, I saw nothing of their origin, even when they sounded so close to my person.

It was the wailing which finally prompted me to knock upon the chambers of Lord and Lady Fawksby. The house was alive with the sounds of the damned and I was at a loss as to their source.

What began as a resonant moan, which one could easily mistake as the sound of the wind billowing over the tops of the chimney pots, soon developed into a chorus of screams and lamentations the likes of which would unnerve even the hardiest soul. Lord Fawksby answered my furtive knocking, his face ashen with terror. "I have heard naught as harrowing as the wails that have shaken these walls this night!" he began. "Come, we must return Margaret to her resting place above the mantel."

I agreed, for whatever manner of horror afflicted us showed no sign of waning. The two of us hurried through the darkened corridors of Burton Agnes Hall, beset on all sides by ferocious rappings, the crashing of doors and a cacophony of anguished cries. Leaving the hall, it was a relief to be outside, free from the sombre mood that had befallen the manor house with the advent of darkness, if only temporarily. The shrieks and crashes that gripped the house could still be heard as we made our way deep into the gardens, and my thoughts turned to those still in the house, those who must have been cowering in their beds, afraid to peek out from beneath their blankets.

Lord Fawksby led me first into a barn, then to an upturned bucket. "Here," he said, lifting the tin pail, "take her back inside." Only nothing lay beneath. Curses flowed from his lips as he searched the barn. "Dammit, boy, you said you had placed her beneath an upturned pail! Yet she is not here? Will this madness continue until it drives us from our home?"

I joined the search, remarking that it might be possible another bucket was the hiding place of Margaret's skull. After a further ten minutes of searching, Lord Fawksby cried out. "Success! Come, let us return! Jasmine shall be at her wits end, no doubt!"

As we carried the skull of Margaret back inside, an instant hush settled upon the manor. Lord Fawksby and I stood a moment, unnerved by the sudden calm. Moments before, chaos had raged within these walls. Now all was still. Lord Fawksby made his way towards the great hall and I followed, eager to see Margaret returned to her rightful place, grateful that we might be able to savour a moment's peace before dawn. With shaking limbs, Lord Fawksby placed her skull onto the centre of the mantelpiece, back in the position where she had long held court.

What followed was a curious feeling. The mood lightened the moment she touched the wood of the mantel. It was then that I noticed the first rays of sunlight piercing the ill-fitting drapes, and heard with a sense of welcome relief the opening notes of the dawn chorus.

✣

The night's events were discussed at length during breakfast (which was taken later than usual due to the disturbed night that all occupants of the house had suffered). Lord Fawksby appeared the more shaken of our number. I assumed he felt an air of blame in regard to our torment, as it was he who had arranged for this experiment to be carried out. Both Lady Fawksby (who seemed utterly fascinated with the night's events) and I explained that he need not feel he ought to take any form of accountability.

I concluded that despite my best efforts, I could find no rational explanation for what we had endured during the night. Though at first I had been confident that I could at the very least attribute the heavy footfalls to a person or persons actively wandering the house, this was not the case. Throughout my searches at the height of the disturbances, I had failed to apprehend anybody.

Again, with regard to the wailing, which I had initially attributed to the wind, I concluded that this was not its origin, given the variety, volume, location and content of sounds heard. There had been a human element behind the majority of the sounds. Genuine emotion, that of anger and torment, had carried through the halls. Occasional words had been heard such as *lament, love, return* and *family*. These I could not satisfactorily explain away.

Nor the rapping and the slamming of doors. For frequently they had occurred in several locations at once. I was confident that should hoaxers have been at large within the manor, I would have caught sight of them at some point during the night.

I advised that for the time being, in order to keep an air of calm in the hall, the skull of Margaret Anstey remain on the mantelpiece.

❖

That was not the last I saw of Lady Jasmine Fawksby. Little did I foresee the profound influence that she would have upon me. Alas, those are tales for another time.

In our first correspondence (of which there were many), she informed me that her husband had taken to excavating a nook behind the top of the mantelpiece, in which the skull was soon interred. The remains of Margaret reside there still. There have been no further reports of disturbances occurring in or around the manor house to date.

Six

THE DEVIL AND THE HILL

Silbury Hill, Avebury, Wiltshire, March 1872

Not all of my investigations came to me by way of personal invitation. I spent many an hour conducting research in some of the finest libraries this country has to offer. For as my experience grew, so did my desire for further knowledge. Folklore and mythology are vast topics; only now dare I venture that I possess a decent degree of knowledge on each. It was during one such visit that I came upon the tale of Silbury Hill.

Situated near Avebury in the county of Wiltshire, Silbury Hill is widely regarded as the largest man-made earth mound in Europe. Dating from around 2500 BC and composed primarily of chalk, it was long believed to be a burial mound. Though no records exist to indicate why the mound was constructed, the architects of such a site clearly deemed their monumental efforts worthwhile. As you may well imagine, tales abound as to its origin and contents.

Lodging in the nearby village of Beckhampton afforded me the luxury of meeting those who had grown up in the shadow of the monolithic mount. I heard a great many colourful stories from the villagers with regard to their experiences around the hill, yet each story held, at least, one recurring element. I shall present the version which most captured my imagination, told in the words of Trapper Jim (as he preferred to be known).

"That ol' hill been 'ere longer than time isself. Folk'll try and tell yer it marks the grave of some fancy king, but I'll tell yer now… ain't nothing buried beneath that place. Truth is, that ain't the work of no man. 'Tis Lucifer who built that hill, and folk round 'ere will attest he's still seen on it some nights. I seen 'im meself!

"The Almighty cast him from the heavens, but yer know that from the Good Book, no? The Devil, he was ner happy at having to leave paradise, so one night, he climbed outta hell, emerging right where Silbury Hill now stands. With a plot in mind, he began to dig into the earth. They say one time this were all forest—till he came along and tore it all up, that is. All through the night he laboured, building Silbury Hill with handfuls of mud and clay. Finally, exhausted from his efforts, he climbed to the top of the hill and began to scream unholy sentiment towards the heavens. For seven days and seven nights he did bellow at the skies, and God replied with storms o' anger and floods o' rage, all of which helped shape the land as you see it now.

"On the eighth day, the Devil quietened, returning to his throne in the fiery depths o' hell. Some say on a stormy night, if yer strain your ear against the din of the wind, ye shall surely hear him curse the heavens. I have, an' like I said, many round 'ere have also. 'Tis the Devil's mound, that place. Go, see for yesself."

✣

Silbury Hill was but a short way from the village, and I made the journey in good time. A small boy by the name of Jonas insisted upon following me along the way. Amongst the many things he spoke of during our relatively short walk, he informed me that he was nine years of age, he had an older brother who teased and beat him daily and he was not much taken by the broth served by his mother.

It was dusk by the time I had settled upon an adequate spot from which to observe the coming night's activity of Silbury Hill, and the sun had already concluded the majority of its westerly descent. The mound itself stood in the centre of a large field, which was populated with a herd of cows. I noted that none of the animals (and to my eyes, there numbered well over a hundred) ventured within thirty yards of the base of the hill.

As night settled upon Jonas and me (for the boy had yet to tire of my silence), a sudden panic set amongst the herd. The cows began to low and pace back and forth, the chorus of their bellows gaining in volume until the flock dispersed all at once and headed towards the perimeter of the field. There was no way out of the pasture that I could see, though I concluded there must be a gate located somewhere, likely hidden from sight by the thick hedgerow that surrounded the field. The cows, now galloping at a considerable speed, thundered towards the hedges that penned them in, and with a level of agility seldom expected of such creatures, leapt into the adjoining greens.

Jonas and I watched the field before us empty as pockets of cattle sought sanctuary in the smaller surrounding meadows. "I've heard Farmer Paul moan about this," began the boy. "He says his cows often run off, and he doesn't bloody know why!"

I reminded Jonas that it was not becoming for a young boy to use such language and suggested he might wish to return home. The actions of the herd had unnerved me. Something unseen had spooked the animals, and I concluded that this might not be the best place for a young boy to be. He quietly ignored my suggestion and began to beat the tall grass that lined the sides of the lane with a long stick he had procured earlier that day. "Me mam won't care if I'm back late," he claimed. "She says it lets her get on with her needlework that way."

❖

Silent hours passed in which I observed the moon sliding across the sky. I welcomed the nightly rebirth of the stars, and I listened to the comings and goings of various nocturnal animals. Jonas continued to entertain with a series of stories about his older brother and the misadventures that usually followed until eventually he grew weary, curled himself into a small ball and settled into a light sleep. Aside from the bovine exodus hours earlier, little of note had occurred, and I felt my eyelids growing heavy. The gentle snoring of the boy, the subtle flutter of the stars and the unseasonably warm air of spring hastened me towards slumber.

❖

It was the heat that woke me—it came at first as a gentle lapping, as though I were dozing next to a roaring fire, which my mind reminded me I was not. Jonas was still asleep. I climbed to my feet. The wave of heat lightly stroked at the right side of my face. It was radiating from the area of Silbury Hill.

I turned. There on the hillside shone a pillar of flame and, within it, the outline of a figure. The light emitted by the apparition illuminated half of the hill and more! The heat made the air shimmer, and the image of the flaming figure began to waver and warp. I called to Jonas, who did not reply. A quick glance down revealed he was no longer sleeping. Instead, I caught sight of him fleeing back towards the village, a mud-spattered pair of bare heels glowing in the moonlight.

Again I was overcome with a sense of curiosity, one which drove me forwards, regardless of fear or logic. Though the temperature began to climb with every step towards the flaming figure, I followed him up the hill. As I drew nearer, I was forced to slow my pace or else collapse under the weight of the intense heat. I heard the air begin to crack and tear, such was the temperature on the hill. My clothes started to smoulder, and my hair proceeded to smoke. The flaming figure was but twenty yards ahead of me, oblivious to my presence, but I realised I could get no closer without exposing myself to danger.

The figure in flames reached the peak of the hill and stood for a moment, before shrieking at the night. The meaning of the words uttered was lost, such was the intensity of the voice that cried them. I pressed my hands to my ears, fearing I might lose my hearing entirely! As the last syllables of his cry faded, the figure began to melt into the earth.

Feeling the air cool and with ringing in my ears, I began to pick my way up the hillside, eager to reach the summit before the spectre disappeared entirely. Alas, I was not so fortunate, for when I reached the top of the mound, naught remained but a small circle of charred grass.

⸙

This was the first investigation (of but a few) where I had found little in the way of answers. Perhaps that is why it is so easily called to mind? I do not like to leave an investigation no better for having started it, yet occasionally this comes to pass. Though the story with which Trapper Jim had regaled me was indeed colourful and entertaining, what I witnessed on the hillside that night was no Devil. So, I ask, who was the soul destined to forever march to the peak of Silbury Hill aflame, and what of his torment? I conclude that we might never know, for the tale of his origin seems to be lost in the annals of time.

To this day, I have yet to identify the apparition, though sightings of The Flaming Man (as he has come to be known locally) continue to be reported.

Seven

THE HANDS OF EVIL

The road to Dartmoor, 1876

L et us return to the journey I discussed earlier and continue with our story as I explore one of the most desolate regions of our country.

Dartmoor is a damnable place. Her windswept moors offer little but misery and despair for anyone unfortunate enough to become lost within her. Many a traveller has lost his way and disappeared within her boundaries. The moors seldom return a body.

My interest in this wretched place concerned an alarming story regarding a set of disembodied hands! Now, by this time I had been privy to all manner of weird and fantastical stories, but a pair of hands without a body? And a malicious pair at that! For all reported sightings spoke of beatings, assaults and even murder.

Pity the driver, then, who having already been forced to assist in an unconventional burial in the village of Colyton, was then subjected to a vicious attack from said disembodied hands.

That day the moors played host to a fierce wind. The rain lashed hard against the sides of my carriage, which swayed and bobbed as though we were travelling not along a road, but upon the turbulent North Sea. Suddenly and without warning, the carriage veered sharply to the right and tipped onto its side. I was thrown from my seat and landed hard on my shoulder. Aside from that impact, I was unhurt. Above the roar of the rains, I could hear the whinny of the horses and the cursing of my driver. Miraculously, it seemed that neither of us had been seriously harmed.

With great difficulty, I managed to climb free of the carriage interior and out into the downpour. My driver busied himself releasing the horses from their reins so that they might right themselves in the mud. I assisted as best I could, though not being practised in the workings of a stagecoach, I fear my fumbling efforts actually hindered our progress. One of the horses had broken a leg. It was with a great degree of sadness that I watched my driver end his suffering, the crack of the pistol momentarily piercing the din of the storm.

My driver led, holding the reins of two of the horses, one in each hand. I followed with the remaining horse. Neither of us engaged in conversation, for the ferocity of the tempest all but stole our words as soon as they were spoken. It was better to save our breath. Tired and weather-beaten, we pushed on along the track.

✧

We walked most of the night before chancing upon a small coach house named The Ne'er Taken. Mercifully, a light shone from within, and after a few minutes' knocking we roused the innkeeper. Fatigued, we stabled the horses before making our way into the empty bar, where our kindly host had set a fire for us. After a quick change of clothes and a bowl of warm soup, I elected to question my driver as to how we had come to find ourselves upturned in a ditch.

"I know it weren't me," he began, his eyes wide with certainty. "I've driven through worse, sir, much worse. Faster too! It weren't the horses neither. I know the weather was rough an' all, but they've seen rougher. They weren't spooked or nothing."

I pressed him further.

"If you'll pardon me for saying, sir, this journey has been naught but mither! I've made a pretty penny like, but after tonight, I'm thinking of staying in the city and doing short runs. I've had my fill of the countryside, I reckon." He took a sip of whiskey, and it was then I noticed that his hands were trembling. "I don't know what to say, sir," he continued. "I was holding the reins, tight as always in a storm. I could see the road ahead; the horses were calm…and then…" He paused, searching for the right words. "And then… well, bugger it…someone else's hands took over!"

I asked him what he meant by this.

"It weren't my hands. For a start, I was wearing gloves, see!" He produced a pair of wet leather gloves from his jacket pocket and placed them on the table. "These hands weren't mine. They were big. Real big. And hairy! I saw them…felt them grip mine. I thought my hands were being crushed, it hurt so bad. Then the hands yanked the reins hard right and off we went."

When I asked as to whom the hands belonged, he could offer no satisfactory reply. "They didna belong to anyone, sir! There was no one behind me; there's no room for anyone behind me anyway.

I didna even see any arms. It makes no sense, not to me it don't."

I thanked him for explaining and fetched him another whiskey in the hope it would calm his nerves. Never had I seen such a man so shaken. I assured him that I believed his story and that he was not to blame for the accident. "But the hoss, I had to end it for him. I've never had to do that until tonight. Poor thing, it's no way for an animal to go. We shall have to bury him on the morn."

I agreed that we would and turned to the innkeeper to enquire as to the possibility of lodging.

"Yer had a run-in with John Cutter then, lad?"

I asked the innkeeper to elaborate, citing that we had seen no one on the road save for ourselves.

"I heard the fella there, he was talking about them hands, weren't he?"

I nodded.

"So you did meet Cutter, or what's left of him anyways."

The innkeeper placed a shot of whiskey before me and continued.

"Drink up. You'll be needing this. Yer can thank me after. Few meet Cutter and live to tell the tale. He's a real pest in these parts. Trade has trailed off since word got out about his deeds. We don't see too many folk this way nowadays. I tell yer, he'd be better off in jail than running free on the moors."

The innkeeper proceeded to tell me how a local sculptor by the name of John Cutter had taken to robbing coaches that traversed the moors (due to being unable to sell enough of his sculptures to feed his family), and how he was eventually apprehended. As he had become known as a highwayman of some regard, it was decided that an example be made of Cutter, and his hands were removed. His freedom was returned, but handless and unable to work, he soon lost his home. His family, now disgraced, turned their backs on him, and he ended up roaming the lonely moor roads, begging for coin. Such was his infamy, all who met the handless man knew his identity and of his crimes. Few spared him their breath, let alone a coin or two. It was not long before Cutter inevitably starved to death. He was found dead by the side of the road, the very road which my driver and I had traversed earlier that night.

With no money to his name, he was buried by a group of villagers in an unmarked grave near to where he had been found. It is the stretch of road which passes his grave where incidents involving the severed hands of John Cutter are reported at their highest.

"He died penniless and angry," continued the innkeeper. "Jail might have spared his life—spared us all, I say. Anyway, his hands take what they want now. He has attacked many, women and children too, and he brought you off the road tonight, make no mistake about it. Maybe it's his way of getting his own back on those that robbed him of his livelihood; maybe old habits die hard. All I know is you won't get me travelling those roads at night, not for love nor money."

✣

The next morning, partially revitalised by a few hours' sleep in comfortable beds, my driver and I set off for the wreckage of our coach with the story of John Cutter still fresh in our thoughts. The moors looked no more welcoming by light. A dense fog had settled, meaning that visibility extended no further than a few yards. There was no birdsong, nor wind. The moors were still, save for the two shadows who dared venture into the fog.

❖

The carriage lay in pieces by the side of the road. The damage inflicted looked far worse by day than we had imagined. My suitcase lay open, its contents strewn across the way. Torn pages from my notebooks, sodden with rainwater, flitted and twisted on the whim of the light morning breeze. Occasionally a sudden gust would lift one of my papers, and I would give chase, only to admit defeat when it was swallowed by the fog. The remains of the horse were gone.

"Where the hell is she?" said my driver. "Who'd have taken her in a storm like that?"

I studied the area where the horse had lain and noticed a series of tracks in the mud, which indicated that she had been dragged from the site of the crash. Of footprints, I could find no sign.

The two of us gathered up what we could carry and headed back to the inn. We would arrange for a second coach to collect us, with the intention of returning to Bristol. Whether or not it had been the ghost of John Cutter who had claimed the carcass of one of our horses and forced us into a ditch the night before went unproved. The moors would keep their secret that day.

Eight
FATHER

It is no secret that my choice of path caused a significant degree of friction between my father and me, though the issue was never spoken of at great length. He was a proud man, and with every right. Having established himself in the textile industry at an early age, he went on to become one of the nation's leading suppliers of high-quality materials, receiving a royal commendation to recognise his hard work. That he should be upset that I, his only heir, chose not to follow him into the family business was to be expected.

I recall one evening he entered my study, which was most unusual as he and I seldom crossed paths, though we dwelt in the same house. (At this time I had yet to make enough of a fortune to purchase a property, and as my family home afforded me the comforts I required, I ruled out the idea of renting, preferring to work towards securing a place of my own). I was working on a set of case notes, I forget regarding what exactly, and I did not divert from my work, save to acknowledge his presence. For a time, he walked the floor of my study, pausing intermittently to scrutinise a particular book from my collection or to examine one of the numerous artifacts I had amassed during my troubles. It was while he inspected a mourning brooch that he spoke. "What is it that you seek, scrabbling around the darkened countryside? Surely it is not success?"

I set aside my pencil. The directness of his question had caught me unprepared, and his expectant glare informed me that he required an honest and intelligent answer. I always assumed that my father saw success as measured in wealth and prestige, and it was these issues I opted to address. "I shall certainly not be involved in the work that I do for financial gain, for what little coin I am paid pales in significance to the fortune I could have acquired had I opted to follow in your footsteps."

He placed the brooch back onto the bookshelf and turned to face me. It was the first time I had ever seen the ravages of age in my father's features. His skin was pale; his eyes were circled by dark shadows, and his hair seemed limp and colourless. "It is not money that measures the worth of a man, son. It is what he has done for those around him. Whether he chooses to help others or to help himself. Standing and influence count for nothing if you do nothing but fill your own pockets."

I had never heard my father speak so openly before, and any notion I had held regarding truly knowing the intricacies of my father's temperament disappeared. Though he was a man of few words, my assumptions about what drove him in his work had been proven incorrect. It was then that I realised he and I were more alike than I had dared to imagine. "I do this to help, in what little a way may transpire. I try to bring understanding. I try to dispel fear. Yes, sometimes I fail. Sometimes I am challenged by forces that I cannot possibly ever hope to understand, yet I am driven to try… to better myself with more knowledge, so that when a community or an individual reaches out to me, I can help the best that I can."

A whisper of a smile crossed those aged lips of his. "And what do you mean to achieve…in the long term, I mean?"

I admit, this was not something towards which I had dedicated much thought, and his question began to stir ideas that I had only previously entertained in passing. "I don't know. I wish to continue with my work, for I have developed a passion for it that no other occupation can hope to replace. Perhaps a book, or a series of books, documenting my work for future generations."

"My son, the author."

"Perhaps, in time. When I have enough material."

Seemingly satisfied, he made his way towards the door. He walked with a stick and a pronounced limp. How had I not noticed this before? My work had apparently captured my attention far more than I had realised. He paused at the door, his hand hovering over the doorknob. "They are all laughing at you, you know. The families, the boys whom you schooled with, in their proper jobs and their grand houses."

Though I knew this statement likely to be true, a pang of disappointment struck my gut. "I care not what they say."

Leaving the study, he spoke only a solitary word. "Good."

Nine

THE HOUNDS OF WISTMAN'S WOOD

West Dart, Dartmoor, Devon, November 1872

The incident with the hands of John Cutter was not my first foray into Dartmoor, nor was it to be my last. My initial excursion consisted of a visit to one of only three high-altitude forests in the county, a place known to locals as Wistman's Wood, so named from the local dialect *wisht*, meaning eerie.

I am familiar with the writings of Dante, and it was his work which played upon my mind as I crossed into the throngs of the dark forest. Though autumn was upon us, no carpet of coloured leaves lay upon the ground. The gnarled oaks that populated this forest had withered and died many years ago. This was a place not a part of the cycle of life, but of death. The air hung stale and silent.

The ground sodden and still. It was clear that no creature made its home in this cursed expanse.

I chanced upon this forest having seen it depicted in a series of oils by artist Meryl Chanter. I was fortunate enough to engage her in conversation at the close of her exhibition, and she told me why she had chosen to paint these particular woods.

"I find beauty in the most desolate wastes. An Englishman might spend his whole life never knowing what wonders lie beyond the hills that border his home. It is my desire to bring the forgotten world to attention."

She continued to explain her fascination with Wistman's Wood.

"This is a place not easily reached, for it lies on the banks of a mountain, or so the climb would have you believe. Little thrives here. There is a beauty in its solitude that I was driven to capture on canvas. It is said that the countess of Devon, Lady Isabella de Forz, planted the forest shortly before her death. Legend has it that the oaks grew into the intricate shapes we see today out of sorrow. You see, the forest's one wish was that her creator would see her in bloom. Alas, this was not to be. Few locations have remained with me quite so acutely as Wistman's Wood."

Her paintings conveyed a sense of loss seldom committed so profoundly to canvas. I purchased one of the oils of the forest and it remains hanging in my office to this day.

I lingered, my painting under my arm, until the crowds had dispersed and the gallery was to close. It was then that Meryl recounted the story which instigated my visit.

"There is another legend attached to the woods," she began, "though I must forewarn you that this tale is ripe with dread. There was once a farmhand smitten with his master's daughter, but the master of the house was fiercely opposed to their friendship. Unperturbed, they continued to see one another using Wistman's Wood as a meeting place. The forest provided them with secrecy, affording them a private place where they could be together, far from prying eyes. In time, their relationship blossomed.

"One night, the farmhand returned to the home of his master, alone and covered in blood. Overcome with shock, when pressed, he babbled about the hounds of the night coming out of the darkness and snatching his beloved from his arms. In an effort to save her, he took her by the hand before turning to flee. Free of the forest and far from the baying of the hounds, he turned, only to find all that remained of his lover was the bloodied stump of her forearm. This he then produced for his master to see.

"The master ordered a thorough search of the forest and its surrounding area, yet no sign of his daughter was found. With no body recovered and only the far-fetched testament of a frightened boy upon which to make a decision, the master, overcome with woe, deduced that the boy had slain his daughter in a fit of rage and had buried her remains somewhere within the woods. The farmhand was hanged from an oak on the edge of the thicket, and his body interred beneath.

"It is said that should you dare the forest when the moon rises high and full, you will hear the baying and howling of the hounds, who, catching wind of your scent, shall hunt and devour your soul. Indeed, many a traveller has entered those woods and failed to leave. No sign of their bodies is ever found; such is the curse of Wistman's Wood.

"I admit that I saw no sign of any such beast during my visit, but then I only ventured into the copse during the light of day.

After all, I can only paint by light. Come nightfall, that is a place in which I would fear to tread."

✧

Lit by the full moon and suffering the bite of a stiff, easterly wind, I felt my decision to venture into the woods had been ill-advised. Alone save for my notebook and a gaslit lantern, I traversed the twisted paths that crossed the grove. My eyes proved useless, as did my light, for naught could be seen beyond a few feet in either direction. I swear I had never experienced a truer sense of loneliness before this night.

Though I cannot be sure, for the long hours spent in that dreary place may have toyed with my senses, I do believe I heard the sounds of dogs close by. Intermittently, between gusts, when the wind faltered to stillness, gathering its strength for the next mighty blow, then and only then did I hear the bass growl of a nearby dog, low and threatening. Eyes upon me I did sense, yet I could observe no movement, save for the disturbance caused by my own clumsy footfalls.

Come dawn, a wave of relief swept over me the likes of which I can scarcely describe, and I picked my way down the hillside wholeheartedly, keen to return to the hustle of civilization away from the dread of the woods.

Is it for me to say that Wistman's Wood holds more than a collection of decaying oak and an atmosphere of dread? Of that I cannot be sure. Suffice to say it would only be the foolish or the naïve who would brave to set foot within her cursed grounds after dark.

Ten

THE ABDON BOGGART

Abdon, Shropshire, January 1873

I t was the height of January and nary a day escaped the touch of a lingering frost or a gentle flurry of snow. I had elected to remain indoors and dedicate my time to the writing up of case notes, having fallen considerably behind with the paperwork which accompanies each investigation. Knowing that I ought not to be disturbed, Mother came quietly into my study clutching a letter. Having become accustomed to my practices, she placed the sealed envelope on my desk and left. Though I knew her to be curious as to the exact nature of my work, she refrained from asking questions.

The letter requested my immediate presence. Penned by the parish vicar, it explained that the farms neighbouring the village of Abdon had suffered a terrible harvest the autumn before and, having assumed this was due to a combination of terrible luck and unseasonable weather, the villagers had turned their attentions towards the next batch of crops. However, it seemed that Abdon's cow herds were being afflicted by a curious ailment that had already led to a significant number of their deaths. Moreover, the milk produced by the cows was already soured upon milking. The vicar hinted at other odd occurrences but explained that they would be better discussed in person. Should I accept the villagers' plea for help, I was to lodge at one of the neighbouring farmhouses and my expenses would be met in full. It was further added that should I be able to isolate the cause of the cattle deaths, then not only would I have the gratitude of the community, but I would receive extra payment.

My initial analysis mainly focused on the possibility that the cows were falling ill due to a new form of disease. Though not medically trained, I concluded that it may well be worth a visit to Abdon, if only briefly, to see if this was the case. Disease shows signs and symptoms that are often missed upon first examination. I wagered I might be able to solve this mystery quickly and set the community to implement preventative measures so that the remainder of the herd be saved. At this point, the possibility of there being a paranormal cause was far from my thoughts.

❖

Abdon is a small, isolated village set on the slopes of Brown Clee Hill, Shropshire. I must admit that the hamlet set among the rolling fields of the Shropshire countryside, sparkling in the winter sun, was truly a sight to behold. It is at times such as these that England reminds you of her beauty and demands your attention. Though I suffered from the cold, I had enjoyed my journey. I listened to the snap of frozen mud cracking beneath the wheels of the carriage, saw countless fields of frosted grass, still and defiant in spite of the crisp breeze. I saw vast forests of bare trees, brooding, silent and brittle with frost. Winter brings a certain serenity to the land and were it not for the cold, which I find unbearable, would be my preferred of the seasons.

The farm which I was to call home for the duration of my stay consisted of a squat, single-storey cottage, a couple of barns and several fields. There was no sign of life save for a cluster of cows grazing in the furthest field.

I unloaded my case and bid my driver farewell. As I watched him depart, a sudden wind whipped between the outhouse and the barn, carrying with it a dreadful stench. I began to gag and reached into my pocket.

There came a voice from behind me. "I'll wager the good vicar never mentioned the smell, right?"

With a fresh handkerchief pressed to my nose, I turned in the direction of the voice. Standing in the doorway of the farmhouse was a young woman. She wore her long blonde hair in a tight ponytail that hung from her shoulder and fell across her breast. Her eyes were warm and overflowed with kindness, her cheeks red and full. She smiled as she spoke again. "Are you gonna stand there all day an' freeze ta death or do you want to come on in?"

I ducked through the small doorway and entered the gloom of the farmhouse. The young woman closed the door behind me and pulled a thick curtain across, hiding the opening from view.

"Fire's lit," she said, pointing to a small wooden stool set to the right of a roaring fireplace. There was no light save for the orange lick of the flames. The few windows the farmhouse offered were covered with the same thick material she had used to hide the door behind. "Keeps the heat in," said the woman, noticing my curiosity. "Father will be back shortly; he went to get some things from up top. Shouldn't be long."

I nodded and thanked her for accepting me into her home. Once the warmth had returned to my bones, I asked her about the deaths of her cattle.

"We had nineteen cows at one point," began the woman as she busied herself at a small sink. "Seth over the way had thirty-two. Now we've seven, and Seth, he's got a couple more than that. Never seen anything like this before. We've had cows sick before an' all, but not like this. Some mornings we woke up to see a line of 'em all dead. Sometimes they're scattered all over. Don't make no sense. Today we didn't lose any, thank the Lord. But until we know what's going on, none of us are gonna sleep well."

She went on to explain that she, her father and Seth provided the village with vegetables and meat. The failed harvest meant that food was already scarce. Losing cattle further added to the communities' worries.

"No one will eat the meat," she explained. "They think it's cursed or something. Then there's that smell. Horrible, right?"

I nodded.

"Comes an' goes. With the sour milk and the other things going on, people are saying we've got a boggart."

I had read several articles on the topic of boggarts but had yet to encounter one for myself. Indeed, the descriptions of the creature varied to such a degree as to almost make it impossible to define what a boggart might possibly be. However, when they were sighted, great misfortune followed, and they quickly became known as omens of bad luck. As to whether or not they existed, I was not entirely sure. Folklore is often crafted to explain (and to warn of) a series of unfortunate events, and though all may have a highly improbable yet logical explanation, the imaginative nature of folklore lends itself well to the memory. This being so, it was no wonder that the misfortune which had befallen Abdon had led some to believe a boggart to be the cause.

I asked the young woman if anyone had seen anything in the area that might resemble a boggart.

"Some have. Or so they say. I've not. Not even sure what to look for. I've heard some say it's hairy; some say it's quick, like a shape that moves so fast you can't ever tell what it really is. One thing they do agree on, though, is that awful stink!"

The door to the farmhouse opened, and an elderly gentleman staggered in, clutching the collar of his coat tightly in a bid to keep out the cold. Beyond him, the wind growled. It took the three of us together to close the door against its might.

Once he had removed his coat, he introduced himself as Abel, said that the young woman was his daughter (but did not offer a name) and joined me by the fireplace. He confirmed that he had dictated the letter I had received and was grateful for my presence. I recited the information his daughter had related in his absence, whilst he nodded and added further details of his own. I then asked him what he had meant when he wrote of those other odd occurrences that would be better explained in person.

"There were the dead cows an' that, an' the smell," he began. "Old Mrs Earnshaw in the village, she says that she's woke in the night by something pulling on her ears. Hard like, enough to tug her outta bed! She says she didn't see who it was, but she sure as heck smelt him! A lot of folks doubted her until we found those tracks."

I asked him what tracks the villagers had found.

"Animal tracks, I s'pose you'd call 'em. Not like any animal I know, mind! Sets of four, big and cloven. I seen 'em near the dead cattle too."

Fascinated, I asked whether he or any of the villagers had ever had the mind to follow the tracks to their place of origin.

"Not bloody likely!" laughed Abel. "That's why we got you in, a fella who knows what he's doing!"

The three of us chatted about village life and the boggart's antics until nightfall, and between us, a plan was devised. Abel and I would keep vigil over his lands that evening in the hope that we might catch sight of something amiss. Should our watch prove futile, we would rest in the day and camp out at night until we witnessed something that might help identify the cause of the curious incidents that had blighted the village.

✤

Our first watch focused on Abel's cattle, and for many an hour, aside from the deathly chill of the night, there was little out of the ordinary to report. Then, as dawn approached, we heard a commotion come from amongst the herd. We rushed across the field as best we were able, though our muscles were stiff and sore from cold. Upon reaching the herd, we found one of its number lying dead upon the frozen mud and a trail of large, cloven footprints circling the area in which the cows had grazed.

Having waited until dawn, we followed the footprints away from the village, down the slopes of Brown Clee Hill, to the marshland that lay to the south-west of the village. It was here that the tracks became lost among the tangle of weeds and sludge so befitting a marsh.

We circled the edge of the wetland, battling against the fierce wind and our fatigue, before eventually concluding that whatever we had tracked to the marshes resided somewhere hidden within its perimeter.

Heading back to the farmhouse to rest, it was decided that Abel and I would recruit the help of Seth, whose farm had also suffered at the hands of the boggart. Abel informed me that Seth owned a "Brown Bess" musket, an heirloom from his grandfather's army days, adding that he thought it might be of use.

I admit that I was uncomfortable with the idea of spending a night on the frozen hillside with a man I barely knew carrying a firearm. My primary concern was that I did not believe a boggart (if such a creature existed) could indeed be shot and killed. Still, I agreed to the idea. I concluded that perhaps the presence of the musket might aid the nerves of my fellow watchmen, if not entirely my own.

❖

That second night was spent pitched on the northern side of the marshes. This particular vantage point was chosen as it afforded a view of the entire marshland.

Hours passed without incident. Abel and Seth filled their time quietly bickering, and despite my urging them to hush, their manner only became more belligerent. I decided that should the investigation extend to a third night, I would conduct the vigil alone.

Suddenly, there came the sound of splintering reeds and the rapid splashing of water. Seth and Abel fell silent mid-argument, and all eyes turned in the direction of the noise. A familiar stench settled upon us. After several seconds of intent listening, I deduced that whatever was moving in the marshes was heading towards us.

Seth, it seemed, had reached a similar conclusion. He stood, began to holler and hurriedly loaded his gun. With Abel egging him on, the pair of them made an almighty din, and it was impossible for me to track the sounds of movement coming from the marsh. I insisted that they fall silent and remain low, but my pleas went unheeded.

A shape, at first featureless, leapt from the weeds and darted towards us. Panicked, Seth unleashed a shot from his musket. The blast of the gun thundered through the silence and the recoil knocked him onto his behind. The flash of the muzzle illuminated our surroundings in an insipid white light, and I saw the creature.

The boggart resembled a German shepherd, only a much larger breed. Its hair was thick, tangled and spattered with mud. It appeared frozen mid-leap due to the split second of light afforded by the gunshot. Where it ought to have had a head, there was only a furry stump. Before I could begin to rationalise what I had seen, darkness swallowed the form of the boggart once more.

Chaos erupted as Abel and Seth struggled to their feet, slipping in the mud, desperate to put distance between themselves and the boggart. With mumbled, nonsensical cries, they turned and headed towards the village. I remained behind. The beast with no head lurked somewhere in the black, its exact whereabouts unclear. I knew it was near, for that same rancid odour still clouded the air. For several minutes, all was still.

With the smell having gradually subsided and satisfied that I was in no immediate danger, I turned towards the farmhouse and followed after Seth and Abel.

❖

At breakfast, I outlined my thoughts to a shaken Abel and his worried daughter. Seth, it transpired, had returned to his home and bolted the door. All attempts to persuade him to open it again had been futile. I explained that the creature we had witnessed on the hillside ought not to exist and that I was at a loss as to how to proceed with dealing with its threat. I informed them that I would need to return home to consult my notes, promising I would return as soon as I had a practical solution as to how to deal with the boggart.

At first, Abel and his daughter were unwilling to let me go, evidently fearing that I might not act on my word. I explained that if I remained with them, I might spend several weeks trying unsuccessfully to drive off the boggart through trial and error. Therefore, it made far more sense to tackle the issue having spent time consulting my library.

Reluctantly they agreed and bid me a fearful farewell, my promise of a hasty return still ringing in their ears.

❖

I set upon my notes with feverish intent, and within a matter of hours had devised a solution I deemed to be practical. I returned the following week, my carriage laden with bags of salt and boxes of horseshoes. Upon disembarking in the village, I gathered up a party of able-bodied men, and between us, we carried the horseshoes and salt bags down the hillside to the edge of the marshlands. There, I instructed that a perimeter of salt be laid around the brink of the marsh and that periodically a horseshoe be placed on the grass.

Soon after, the endeavour was completed. Weary, we returned to the village and headed for the tavern, where I explained my plan to those gathered. Salt was a natural purifier, or so it was believed. Early folklore suggested that a boggart could not cross a line of salt, and by circling the marsh where it dwelled, essentially we had formed a seal. The horseshoes were an added layer of protection; long thought to be objects of luck, iron was believed to keep spirits and unatural things away. What better way to strengthen a seal than with a large dose of good fortune?

The villagers seemed happy with my explanation, and I went home, well paid and confident that the Abdon boggart would trouble the villagers no more so long as the salt barrier remained intact. From that day forwards, I made certain that whenever embroiled in an investigation, I travelled with a core library (and an extensive collection of personal notes) that would enable me to conduct further research without the need to return home.

Over time, the titles which comprised my portable library were swapped and changed, as I found myself absorbing much of their contents due to the frequency of my reading. Now, I carry but one book with me. It resides in my breast pocket. This book contains information and key observations I have made during my investigations. I like to believe now that there is little I might be faced with which would leave me perplexed.

To this day I am yet to hear a single complaint regarding the Abdon boggart and can only assume that the creature remains confined to the marshland, leaving the village to flourish once more.

Eleven

THE ART OF DISBELIEF

Having shared some insight into my work, perhaps now it is time to address my thoughts on scepticism. Scepticism is an integral part of the investigative process. It is an element of my character which at first seems at odds with my motivations, yet it is vital that it remain a part of my psychological constitution.

When I initially began to investigate the paranormal, I had no preconception nor understanding of what I was about to undertake. If you had asked me before my foray into Alverton *did I believe?*, likely I would have laughed and explained that of course I did not believe. At least not entirely. The truth was that I could not believe, not then, when I was so naive to the ways of the paranormal.

I am schooled (to a degree) in the fields of science, mathematics and language, much, I imagine, as are you.

We are taught at a young age that the world is governed by rules and systems so that order may prevail. This is how we come to understand the world and our function within it. Yet what if there are elements which fall outside of these rules and systems? What of the boggarts, the screaming skulls and the mermaids? How are we to interpret their existence if we cannot apply our rules to them?

I digress. Let me put this simply. I believe, though not all tales and never on the strength of hearsay. I have experienced far too many incidents that occur outside of our system of rules not to believe. Yet to conduct an investigation of any worth, one needs to provide proof that lies within the rules of our understanding. If I can supply proof of an event or creature that is accepted and understood by the laws of science, mathematics and language, then I can confidently present my work to an accepting public.

Where many investigators fall foul is in the presenting of evidence that is weak, or worse, falsified, in order to prove their belief. Faith is all well and good in religion, which in my opinion should be viewed in terms of its philosophical merit and not be interpreted as fact. In the field of the paranormal, providing proof that is both logical and factual is the most effective means of conveying a theory or explanation that might otherwise be construed as residing beyond the realms of accepted thinking.

Therefore, maintaining a degree of scepticism when conducting an investigation into the paranormal is crucial. For example, this mindset allows me to identify quickly those witnesses who are fraudulent or have little in the way of valid information to offer. Remaining sceptical means that I follow a diligent and concentrated passage of investigation, and it defines and further hones any conclusions I might reach. The questions born of scepticism invariably help to shape the truth. I learned early to think of each investigation in terms of a large piece of granite, the truth of which lies buried within its core: scepticism is the chisel of truth.

Twelve

THE RESTLESS WITCH

East Mersea, Essex, May 1873

I have already alluded to the fact that Lady Fawksby and I remained in contact long after our meeting at Burton Agnes Hall. We had shared many letters by this date, sometimes as many as four in a month, and I found our exchanges both enlightening and exhilarating. Jasmine was a like-minded soul, as passionate on the subject of the paranormal as I, and able to offer new approaches of thought which I freely admit have helped to shape my work. Such was her appetite for the subject that our letters quickly began to span several pages.

Often, she would direct me towards further reading in regard to stories of strange occurrences that occurred in her county, urging me to travel north so that I may join her on an investigation. Though I repeatedly entertained the idea, I decided it would be better if I remained distant. I would reply in earnest, thanking her for her recommendations but each time politely declining her invitation, citing that I had much to occupy me. Though it pained me to refuse her, she seemed to take my repeated repudiation in good spirit.

I should lie if I claimed that I did not wish to see her again. That I found her enchanting I need not say. The initial spark I had felt upon meeting her resided within me still. Thoughts of her would spark butterflies in my stomach. I had yet to feel anything quite like our connection with anyone else, and I found myself thinking of her often. She stirred a wealth of emotions within me, emotions which I persuaded myself that I ought to forget, for she was wed to another and therefore it was not fitting to want for her in such a way.

See, even now thoughts of her distract!

It was late in April when I received a letter written in a curious, almost illegible hand, requesting my presence on the island of Mersea. The letter explained that the residents of the island were suffering due to the actions of a young girl by the name of Sarah Wrench, who, having died in 1848, still plagued the island every sixth of May, which the letter explained was the anniversary of her burial. The author of the letter asked that I travel at once, bringing with me the means with which to keep a restless corpse safely interred. It was not signed, but there was a forwarding address should I choose to reply.

✣

I found it amusing that Mersea had the audacity to name itself an island. While geographically it is indeed almost entirely surrounded by water, with the Colne Estuary lying to the south and the River

Colne all but completely cutting through the mainland, leaving only a single road as the route into Mersea, passage can be made easily by wading through the shallow river.

I arrived in the small village of East Mersea on the fifth of May. Expecting the author of the letter to be a local resident, I was surprised to be met by Lady Fawksby. After a brief (and awkward) embrace and the exchanging of greetings, I enquired as to what she was doing so far from Burton Agnes Hall.

She explained that it had been she who penned the letter requesting my assistance and that, seeing how I was forever declining her invitations, she had decided to take the initiative and draw me out of seclusion. She had written the letter with her left hand, disguising her handwriting, and had set up a forwarding address so that she might receive my reply. She assured me that the story she had sent was based on truth, and she apologised for stooping to such crooked means to draw my attention.

I assured her that no apology was required and that it was good to be in her company once again. Hearing further as to how set she was upon joining me on the night's investigation, I outlined my plan.

✥

The parish priest, a slight, elderly gentleman by the name of Father Earnshaw, showed Lady Fawksby and me to the troublesome grave. The girl was buried on the north side of the church, the area of the cemetery reserved for sinners and suicides. When pressed as to why Sarah Wrench was interred on this particular side, the priest merely grunted and pointed to a rough patch of upturned earth.

"That's hers," said the priest, making a quick sign of the cross. "See how nothing grows nearby."

The grave lay at the farthest point from the church. The grass surrounding it was withered and black, as though the earth had been scorched. The grave was unmarked.

"Seems a shame that she should lie here without her name attached, don't you think?" said Jasmine.

"You say that now with the benefit of ignorance," began the priest, seemingly taken aback by Jasmine's question. "For though young in years, she was capable of villainous acts. All of which she was tried for, might I add."

"Tried and found guilty, as were so many others," replied Jasmine, a note of sorrow in her voice. "The witch-hunts blight our proud history. Many innocent women died due to the ignorance of man."

"That they did," countered the priest. "But this one had it coming. Even God has no place for her in his kingdom." He turned towards me. "The parish sincerely hopes that you can help contain her curse."

I nodded and assured him that we would do all we could to put the fears of the community at ease.

✣

I suggested to Jasmine that we ought to visit the nearby village to gather accounts of the alleged disturbances, explaining that first-hand accounts, though often littered with contradictions and factual errors, could hold key pieces of information which enabled a better understanding of the forces that might be at work. I remember that she smiled at me, her eyes mischievous and knowing. She positively delighted in telling me she had already spoken to the majority of the villagers, most of whom had been only too keen to tell their tale!

We spent that afternoon in the graveyard, I listening enthralled while Jasmine recounted the stories of the villagers, she delighting in being part of the investigation. I could sense her excitement. It transferred via her movements, the feeling with which she spoke and the look in her eyes. It was those eyes and her scent which stirred those hitherto buried emotions most of all.

We talked about everything and nothing, enjoying those silent moments, natural moments, in one another's company. There was tension between us, pure and light. One that teased at sinful possibilities. I saw that she delighted in it as much as I, and the beginnings of the connection first felt at Burton Agnes Hall developed into a bond that became impossible to ignore. A solitary raven observed us from atop a crooked gravestone, curious yet approving. Those sun-kissed hours spent in the cemetery that day passed in the blink of an eye.

❖

According to the villagers, the aggrieved spirit of Sarah Wrench returned to her body upon the stroke of midnight every sixth of May. The community then spent the next twenty-four hours locked away in the safety of their homes, fearing to set foot outside or else feel the wrath of the vengeful ghoul. Many told that she would move from cottage to cottage, hammering on windows and doors, wailing and screeching, until the toll of midnight the next night summoned her to the grave once more. Those who braved to leave their homes during the anniversary of her burial suffered vicious assault. It was alleged that one poor farmhand had been scared mute! Suffice to say, the villagers lived in fear of the date and hoped that we would be able to help find a solution to their woes.

❖

As dusk gave way to night, I suddenly realised that we had spent the afternoon talking, leaving little time in which to prepare for the evening ahead. I instructed Jasmine to keep a lantern lit and to remain by the grave while I collected the tools and pieces of iron I had requested from the village. The hope was that I might build a structure which would serve as a means of keeping Sarah Wrench in the ground.

The two of us made light work assembling the frame, which, once erected, resembled a skeletal cocoon. In position over the grave, it reached almost to the height of my chin. By the light of Jasmine's lantern, I set upon the cage with my lump hammer and began the arduous task of securing it into the ground.

The moon was high and the midnight hour near by the time I laid down my hammer. Exhausted and sodden with sweat, I collapsed onto the dirt. The top of the cage now stood only a foot or so from the ground; such was the effort I had taken in burying it into the depths of the earth. Satisfied that only a suitably large amount of force could remove it from its foundations, I retired to the north wall of the church.

Jasmine followed with her torch held aloft. She had been a blessing during those long, hard hours. Without her support, I doubt I would have been able to exert myself enough to secure the cage. I was thankful for her company.

The moon hung heavy, full and high among a tapestry of stars. We lay together, Jasmine and I, side by side, gazing to the heavens, each lost in thought. The night was warm and still. The silence carried an air of unspoken promise. I remember turning towards Jasmine only to see her lying upon her side, watching me with a smile on her face. I know not how to explain the next moment, for I am no poet, but I felt her lips, thin and gentle, upon mine. Our kiss seemed at once natural and all consuming. In that single moment, all else ceased to be. At that moment there was only she and I. There was our desire for one another and nothing else. At that moment we were somewhere, I thought, untouchable by man. At that moment, we lay in the heavens.

✢

A kiss is governed by laws unto itself, by which I mean a kiss knows its own duration. I can say with a degree of certainty that the screams of the ghoul trying to claw its way free of the iron cage did little to bring about a premature death of our kiss, though once we realised what was happening, the mood did alter somewhat!

I climbed to my feet and rushed towards the iron cage, urging Jasmine to stay back and away from harm. Sarah Wrench had fought her way to the surface of her grave and was proceeding to thrash and wail, sending mud and soil flying as she desperately tried to escape her new prison.

Panicked, I threw myself onto the cage, hoping my added weight would hinder the ghoul's efforts, but the pen continued to shake and buckle. The strength of the creature was terrifying, as was its fury. I closed my eyes so that I needed not look upon the rotted tangle of flesh that formed Sarah's face. It was then that it dawned on me I may be required to lie on top of the cage until the following night! If indeed I let out any audible kind of groan at this realisation, I am thankful it was likely lost amid the frenzied cries of the ghoul.

I do not know how long I spent riding that bucking, shaking iron cage, as the incessant shrieking of the ghoul seemed endless, but cease it finally did. So suddenly, in fact, that I almost fell off, such was my anticipation of moving to coincide with the next violent jolt.

Jasmine spoke first. Her voice was soft and eerily distant, at least to my ears, which had suffered the raucous screeches of the ghoul. She bid that I open my eyes. With all still and serene once more, I obeyed, only to be greeted by the sight of the macabre frame of Sarah Wrench lying beneath me. Her hollowed eyes locked with mine. Neither of us moved.

"It's quite all right to climb off," said Jasmine. "I wrote a quick blessing and placed it on her cage. It seemed to soothe her, don't you think?"

Having neither the time nor the inclination to argue the merits of what constituted a soothed ghoul, I quickly dismounted the cage and took my place beside Jasmine. She regarded me with a curious look, one of both pity and admiration, should such a conflicted look exist!

I thanked her for her help and stooped to read the blessing. Whatever was written on the scrap of paper that Jasmine had entwined through the bars of the cage had certainly calmed Sarah.

Sarah Wrench, child of light,
May God's forgiveness absolve all of your sins.

"I'll etch it into a piece of wood tomorrow," said Jasmine, placing her hand on my shoulder. "I didn't quite have the time to do so just now…you seemed in need of quick assistance!"

❖

We remained by the side of Sarah's grave until dawn, when I ordered Jasmine back to her lodgings in the village. Reluctantly she agreed, and she spent the day resting. Sarah had not stirred since Jasmine had placed the blessing upon the cage, though her eyes remained open and alert. Several times I observed her tracking the movement of the low-lying clouds that spotted the early morning sky. It seemed wrong of me to bury her while she watched the sky, so I elected to remain by her side until the bell tolled midnight and the curse was lifted once more.

Jasmine joined me at dusk, bringing hot soup, bread, water and a blanket. We huddled together beneath the stars, thankful for one another, until it was time to return Sarah to the earth.

It was slow progress, burying a body through the spaces of the cage, but we covered her as best we were able, a ritual no doubt undertook by the villagers each year. Afterwards, I walked Jasmine back to the village tavern. Though exhausted, physically and mentally, being around her invigorated me. Still, I cannot recall what we spoke about on that walk to the village, or even if we talked at all.

Jasmine asked me to stay with her for the remainder of the night. She even offered her bed to me. As a gentleman, naturally I refused, opting to sleep on the floor. I slept soundly that night, not as a result of exertion but of the company which I kept.

When I awoke the next morning, she was already gone. A handwritten note lay on the bedside table.

My dearest Solomon,
My thanks for letting me join you on one of your many adventures. The memory of this time shall stay with me always.
Yours,
J
X

Crestfallen, I returned to the church to find the parish priest standing over the iron cage. He pointed to the grave of Sarah Wrench. "A little medieval, but I heard that it was effective."

I nodded and gestured to the small wooden plaque that was fixed at the head of the grave before explaining that it was the blessing of God and not the cage that had kept Sarah content and in the ground. Turning to leave, I suggested he remember that.

Thirteen

MOTHER

It was many months before I next heard from Jasmine, despite the regularity of letters I sent. For a time, I was puzzled as to why she had left without saying goodbye, and aided by her silence, my mind entertained a number of possible theories. I paid little attention to my work, allowing a collection of cases to amass upon my desk. I had lost my focus.

When finally she did respond, she explained that she had decided to return home without disturbing me, so as not to draw out our goodbye. She stated that she had experienced much in those couple of days that she did not fully understand, citing that distance had allowed her the means and the time to appreciate her emotions. Her place was with Fawksby, and any feelings she may or may not have towards me were better left unexplored. She finished the letter by asking that I not contact her again.

I was heartbroken. Of course, I understood that she was a lady, married to a lord, and as a lady had certain duties and responsibilities to uphold, all of which weighed heavily upon her. Yet that night in the cemetery I had seen her free of her burden, perhaps for the first time since her courtship began. Moreover, I had allowed myself to fall in love with her. This had been foolish, that I knew, yet the heart pays no heed to titles or logic. I had dared dream that she had loved me in return. Her letter implied much to the possibility, though I knew I would likely never find out if this were true.

Those initial days after reading her letter remain grey and indistinct. Time passed by in cumbersome lurches, I a reluctant observer to the world around me. In short, I withdrew into myself. It was my mother who intervened, eventually freeing me of my grief.

She entered my study entirely unannounced. The curtains were still drawn: she threw them aside, chastising me as she did so. The morning light flooded my study, burning my eyes. She stood before me, arms folded, a look of displeasure on her face.

With our pleasantries out of the way, talk quickly turned towards the issue clouding my mood. I gave away little of my mindset, choosing short, curt answers where she hoped I might elaborate.

After a time, annoyed at my stubbornness, citing that it was a trait inherited from my father, she asked of my work. I gave an overview of investigations to date, explaining that I felt I had reached a crossroads. My experience with Jasmine had opened my eyes to a new way of looking at life, and indeed myself. I had no idea how to move forward with my work, nor how to understand the heartache I felt over Lady Fawksby.

My mother turned to face the window. At first, I thought I might have upset her, and I stood so that I might comfort her. She bid me sit, and I obliged. With her form presented to me in silhouette, she began to speak.

"I never questioned your choice of path, nor shall I try to persuade you to continue. Though there is something which I must share with you. Now, having seen something of the unnatural, you will not look upon me as a fool. Your father…he would not understand, and though he would never admit to it, talking about such matters would merely unearth buried pain." She turned towards me and smiled. "You had a sister. Her name was Victoria. She passed shortly after her birth. She was your twin."

Hearing her words elicited a strange and complicated series of emotions, all of which I seemed to feel at once. There was the sense of love and loss felt in a single moment. Victoria, my twin, had lived only a few minutes, and I would never know her.

"I know she passed away," continued Mother. "But she is with us…with you, still."

The air was charged with emotion. Swallowing hard, I asked her to explain what she meant.

"Do you ever feel a presence with you? When all seems at its darkest and hope is lost, do you feel that your burden, your fears—do you feel that they lift somehow? If only a little? Do you hear someone speak to you only to find that no one is there? Does someone point you towards something on some of your investigations that perhaps you earlier overlooked? That is Victoria. She walks with you still. She sees that you are looking into her world, and she hopes that one day you shall see her."

I mulled over the words of my mother and urged her to sit. She took a handkerchief from her sleeve and began to dab at the corners of her eyes. Yes, there were times when I felt that I was not alone, or I revisited a piece of evidence and suddenly saw the situation in a new light—and then there had been the figure in the mist when I was a child. Yet I had pushed these feelings aside, keen to understand only the tangible.

I told my mother the story of Horatio and the figure in the fog. She sat quietly and smiled throughout. When I had finished, she stated that she believed I had seen Victoria. It was she who had been trying to help my dog and me.

I asked as to why it was that she thought Victoria would appear to me at a similar age to myself and not as an infant.

"I can only make an assumption that as your twin, she is bonded to you in death, much as she would have been in life. You grow old together, you on this plane, she on the other. I see it like this. You walk the same path, yet an unseen obstacle divides you. I shall teach you how to see her—if you are willing to learn?"

Without hesitation, I indicated that I would. She then proceeded to talk me through the steps she required to prepare herself for the acceptance of Victoria's presence.

"I begin by closing my eyes and setting my intention, which is to reach my spiritual guide and to receive messages or advice that she wants to pass my way. My guide is my Great Grandmother Joan. I say to myself inside my head, *my intention is thus*, then I sit quietly and listen to the sound of my breathing, focusing on the movement of my abdomen. I simply breathe, steadily and slowly.

I then imagine tying a silver thread around my waist, just a thin silver strand, about the thickness of a piece of string, and I attach the other end to a leg of the chair. This anchors me to here and to now. It allows me to travel wherever I wish—if I become distracted or lost, I can find my way home by pulling the thread. I then say to myself, *I call up my ancestors, my angels, to help me travel safely*, and in my head I imagine a doorway. Everyone has his own doorway: we create our own when we first travel, and it always has a staircase behind it, going down. We do not travel up to their realm.

"We always meet our guides or spirits in our self-created place, which we walk down to. Down because we are accessing our subconscious. My doorway is in an old tree. I open the door and step onto the staircase, which winds down to the left, anticlockwise. I reach the bottom after ten steps and push open another door, which leads to my special place. It's a green meadow, with trees and a river running across it. I walk, barefoot. It is a summer's day, sunny with a gentle breeze. The more senses I can use while I'm here, the better the experience. My mind is convinced it is real if I add sounds and smells; I urge you to do likewise. I cross the bridge towards a tree, which I can sit under comfortably in the dappled shade. The birds are singing, the leaves are rustling, I can smell flowers. I then invite Joan to talk to me. She may sit and speak to me; she might give me a gift, something symbolic that I must interpret. She might answer my questions. She might heal me, or hold me, touch me or simply sit quietly with me. Each experience is different and intense. When I'm done, I reverse my journey, across the bridge, through the door, up the stairs, and as I arrive at the doorway back to the here and now, I thank my guides, angels and others for their love, their help and for keeping me safe. I sit for a couple of minutes as I come back into my space. I open my eyes and breathe. I'm fatigued and need to be outside a while. This, with practice, can bring Victoria to you too, though she is always near."

I thanked her for explaining her technique and asked of Father and his knowledge of Victoria.

"He feels her loss still but is not gifted in the ways that you and I are fortunate. You have inherited your gifts from my family line. My mother and her mother before were all able to converse with the dead. I chose to neglect my gifts for a long time, until Victoria made her presence known. I find great comfort in that presence, and she is so proud of your work. She wishes to protect you. She showed me what occurred the first time you ventured out into the unknown. As you become aware of her, accept her presence, she shall become more of an influence in your life. Do not fear this, for she offers only advice and protection. She has a love for you, son, love as a brother. I tell you this today because I see your pain. It is right that you learn of her now. It is right that you love her in return."

✥

Mother, having said what she needed, left me to my thoughts. The rest of the day I remained at my desk, mulling over her words. I had a twin sister. She was watching over me, helping to guide me in my work. I could not help but wonder if something inside of me had urged me towards working within the realm of the paranormal, perhaps as a means of reconnecting with Victoria. I wondered if it had perhaps been her will that had influenced me.

✥

This was a confusing time in my life, and for a while, I was not sure what to make of my mother's admission. I concluded that she had told me of my sister so that I might overcome my malaise and focus on my work once more. It also made sense that I ought to learn about my family history at some point, but the notion that Victoria was watching over me with the intention of making contact was an idea that I admit I struggled with. I often wondered what it was she would wish to say to me and if I would care to listen.

Fourteen

THE PALLID ONES

Woolpit, Suffolk, October 1873

The village of Woolpit lies east of Bury St Edmunds in the heart of Suffolk. Upon my return to my work, the first newspaper article which caught my interest came from the *Suffolk Herald* and mentioned said village by means of the testimony of the minister of the Blessed Virgin Mary Church, Father Mark Deeny. He claimed that one of his parishioners (whom he refused to name) had shared with him an extraordinary story concerning a pair of white figures that had been witnessed stalking the surrounding dales.

It was common knowledge among the community that sheep often went missing during the dead of night, never to be found again. It transpired that a spate of recent disappearances had all but depleted the flock of one of the village's prominent farmers, and in a bid to solve the mystery, said farmer had gathered a group of hardy individuals and together they kept watch over the flock.

For three nights, not a single sheep was unaccounted for, and the men were on the verge of giving up hope with regard to finding out what was causing the flock numbers to dwindle. However, on the fourth night, just before dawn, the group saw two small, pale figures take one of the sheep by the head and hind legs and carry it away.

Surprised at the audacity of the thieves, the group of men quickly followed after the pallid figures, who, quite unexpectedly, seemed to *vanish into the ground* some distance ahead of them. A thorough search of the area was conducted, yet no trace was found of the figures or of the missing animal.

Father Deeny explained that those present had no cause to give a fictitious account and that all had attested to seeing the same thing—that the two pale figures had seemed to melt into the ground before them in what was a featureless field. There was no place in which they could have hidden, and the search for them carried on until midday to no avail.

The article continued to explain that sheep were still disappearing from the area and that the villagers were afraid the animals were being stolen by disgruntled hill sprites. Father Deeny concluded by expressing his doubt at this theory.

With my interest piqued, I packed a case and secured a seat on a carriage that was scheduled to depart for Suffolk the next morning.

❖

Tiny, crooked cottages nestled together, forming a line against the fierce winds that rolled unopposed across the featureless Suffolk plains. Scattered farmhouses were dotted either side of the line of cottages, with the church lying far to the east. Beyond that was nothing but tangled grasses, overturned tree trunks and muddy bogs. Truly, Woolpit was a desolate place.

Father Deeny, though a shade nervous of my presence, verified that to his knowledge the story I had read was a genuine and accurate account of the one reported to him. Further, he confirmed that sheep were continuing to be lost and that the threat of starvation hung over the village due to the prediction of a harsh winter. When pressed to join me on my investigation, he politely declined and advised that I save my breath when it came to asking any of the villagers. Fear, he explained, was rife among them.

I took to the land where the figures had reportedly been seen, examining it thoroughly in the hope of finding footprints I could track. The turn of the soil and the tangle of the grass made it all but impossible to distinguish animal prints from man's, and I soon abandoned the idea, choosing to focus my search within the area Father Deeny had earlier marked out as where the pale figures had seemed to vanish. It was here that I found the first burrow.

Oval in appearance and larger than that of a badger set, the hole lay covered by thick tufts of grass and would have been easily missed had I not twisted my ankle by stumbling into it. Ignoring the pain, I noted that while it was not large enough for an adult to enter, an adolescent or child might fit comfortably. If the pale shapes had been those of children (and by all accounts, judging by the description of their stature, this could indeed have been the case), then they might have hidden in this hole, appearing to their pursuers to have vanished into the earth.

As I sat and strapped my ankle (using my sock as a makeshift support), I caught the touch of a gust of wind escaping the hole.

This, I deduced, meant that my initial assessment of the gap had been incorrect, for if there was air flowing from it, then that meant there was another entrance.

I sat for a while and listened to the wind as it turned underground. After a time, I arrived at the conclusion that I sat at one of many entrances to a vast network of tunnels. I reasoned it might be that the individuals who were stealing the sheep had not been found because they retreated below the surface, where they could easily conceal themselves in a subterranean warren that the villagers likely knew nothing about.

Convinced that the pale figures witnessed stealing sheep were not apparitions (as many of the villagers believed) but a collective of individuals who hid beneath the ground as a means of escape, I decided to look for an entrance to the arrangement of caverns that I might be able to pass through, to try to locate the culprits. Looking back now, it is easy to say that I ought to have been less hasty in my actions, for I had paid little thought to the possible dangers I might face exploring underground. Surely it would have made sense for me to first return to the village, inform the locals of my discovery and explain my intentions before attempting to gather a party of men to join me. Alas, the excitement of my discovery all but blinded me to any possible danger, and having located a hole large enough for me to pass through while pressed to the ground, I entered the subterranean labyrinth.

As one might imagine, it was dark inside the tunnel, yet not so dark that I was unable to see where I was going. There grew a type of lichen which shone with a faint grey light. I took comfort from its presence as I crawled deeper underground.

There was an odour here, familiar and unpleasant. The tunnel twisted, turned, rose and fell in elevation. Within moments, despite my conscious effort to track my route mentally, all sense of direction was lost. The tunnel was lined with countless smaller passages which branched off at irregular intervals on all sides. The constant drip of water was the only accompanying sound above the struggle of my movement. My breath came shallow and fast. My clothes were soaked and my muscles burned. The fetid smell of death grew more pungent the deeper into the gloom I moved. I lost all sense of time. It may have taken me minutes to reach the intersection where I was able to climb to my feet and stoop, or it may have been hours. Suffice to say, the cramped conditions and the absence of light were beginning to dull my senses.

❖

It started as a mere irritation. An irregular clicking that seemed to sound on all sides, almost unnoticed at first. Yet as my ears grew accustomed to the acoustics of the tunnel, I was alerted to the fact that the source of the clicking came at once from several locations nearby and seemed to shift, unseen in the darkness.

I paused for a moment and focused my attention on the noises that baited me. I could feel the air push over my flesh, carrying with it droplets of moisture and the scents of the earth. As I paused, so too did the clicking sounds. For a moment, I wondered if the nature of my confinement had led to my mind playing tricks on me and I doubted I had heard any such sounds at all.

Remembering that I carried matchsticks, I removed them from my pocket, drew one and struck it alight using the coarse side of the box. A fierce orange flame threw limited light upon my surroundings, and it was then that I saw the pallid face, mere inches from my own, staring back at me from the gloom.

The figure in front of me baulked in fear of the flame and within moments had scuttled away, seeking refuge in a darker corner of the passage. While only afforded a brief view of the creature, I still remember her features, such was the shock of her presence.

She was undoubtedly human, though I must admit that I had never before looked upon such a pitiful cretin as she. Her skin was beyond pale, and her eyes, colourless as they were, held no sign of humanity. It was as though she held no colour within her flesh whatsoever. Her hair, limp and lifeless, which I would describe as white—though it held hardly any hue at all—plastered her neck and shoulders. Her frame was slender, her bone structure clearly visible to my eye. She wore nothing in the way of clothing, her flesh a coat of mud and grime. She was, however, highly agile. Having seen the speed and grace of her movement as she retreated from the flame, I would have found it hard to believe that such a fragile creature might be capable of such movement, had I not witnessed so firsthand.

In the short time that the match burned, I saw the creature before me retreat into the shadows and caught the sound of movement to my left. A chorus of frantic clicks passed back and forth from the shadows, and I deduced that this was how the creatures communicated. As to what they were speaking of I dared not imagine.

The match sputtered out, and darkness closed around me once more. Almost at once I heard hurried movement as the creatures that had fled the light of my match left their hiding places and inched towards me.

With my bearings well and truly lost and panic beginning to set in, I fumbled for my matchbox, the contents of which spilled to the floor. Cursing my luck, I began to back out of the crossway, towards the passage I had emerged from. It is not an easy task to manoeuvre oneself backwards, while crouched, surrounded by darkness and fearing for one's life!

Again, I cannot say how long it took me to navigate back along the tunnel; suffice to say I moved more quickly backwards than I had done forwards earlier that day! The creatures making the clicking sounds did not pursue—at least, I could not say that I saw them nearby. However, I caught the sound of their peculiar chatter several times during my retreat, each time originating from a tunnel or passageway that led off from the one I occupied. Perhaps, then, they did follow? Keen to keep an eye on the imposter from the world above. Eager to make sure that I returned whence I came.

I have no doubt that they could have struck me at any given moment, should they have so wished. I was a stranger in their domain, lost in their home. Why they chose to let me leave that place unscathed, I cannot say for sure, though I need not mention that I was glad to do so.

✥

It was early evening when I emerged, sodden and weary, among the thistles and the grass. I spent the short walk back to the village trying to organise my thoughts. Whatever rationalism I attempted, I knew my story would sound far-fetched. I had encountered individuals living beneath the ground that surrounded the village; that much was true. The descriptions of the sallow creatures seen stealing sheep matched those I had encountered, and I had stumbled upon animal remains during my hasty retreat from their lair. It was evident to me that whoever dwelt underground was using the village's sheep as a source of food. What had happened to prompt them to leave the safety of their lair to forage, I could not say. Though of human origin, these descendants of people had forgone the world and its ways for a life below ground. How else could I explain their gaunt appearance, the means by which they communicated or the extensive network of tunnels, many of which I believed had been dug by hand? Would it be possible for the villagers and those who lived beneath their lands to co-exist? Though I wished it might, I had serious reservations as to whether that would be possible.

I retired to my room after speaking with Father Deeny, assuring him that I would recount my tale to him and his congregation the following morning. That night I slept little, so tormented was I by the ashen face of the creature from beneath the ground.

❖

I shall always hold myself accountable for what they did upon hearing my tale. Gripped by fear of the unknown, and no doubt in part stirred by my inability to provide answers, the villagers took to the fields. Try as I might to deter them from their actions, my pleas fell on deaf ears. Men, women and children sought out places where the creatures I had described might surface, then, in turn, each hole was sealed with a mound of rocks.

Long into the night they worked, and I, helpless to intervene, could only watch in despair. Though I understood the subterranean creatures little, I felt in my heart that they would pose no threat (beyond stealing sheep) to the villagers. Sealing them into the ground amounted to burying them alive. I saw this as an act of murder. Suffice to say the villagers did not.

I left that place the very next morning. Glancing out across the fields, I saw that many of the villagers had returned to the labours of the previous day, such was their commitment to safeguarding their homes from a threat unseen and misunderstood.

I know not what became of the pallid ones, only that I never heard mention of them again. I often wonder whether their knowledge of the underground meant that they were able to escape the attentions of the village and survive unseen elsewhere. Alas, I shall likely never know for sure.

Fifteen

THE SERPENT IN THE LOCH

Urquhart Castle, Scotland, December 1873

My investigation (and the subsequent turn of events) at Woolpit graced the pages of several leading newspapers. Though it is not a case that I look back upon with any degree of warmth, it must be noted that the story of my exploits and those of the villagers travelled far and wide. What followed was a sudden and varied influx of requests through my door. One such letter heralded from the town of Inverness, Scotland, and contained a fascinating claim with regard to one of the country's largest lochs.

The letter came from a respected physician based in Balnain, and described an encounter with an unidentified creature that the author experienced while walking the banks of Loch Ness:

Dear Mr Whyte,

Please forgive my unannounced correspondence, but having seen coverage of your recent endeavours, I trust that you may be the only person who might accept the following tale as fact rather than the ramblings of a madman.

My work inflicts a great deal of stress upon me, and often I retire to the country so that I might clear my mind and invigorate the soul in readiness for the working week. It was on one such excursion to the banks of Loch Ness that I encountered a creature not only unfamiliar to these waters but unfamiliar to these times!

I was walking alone, enjoying the tranquil beauty that only experiencing the loch by dawn can afford, when I heard an almighty churning of water similar to what one might hear with the passing of a large boat. Expecting to observe as much, for often such vessels trawl the loch in search of fish, I turned to look out across the water. It was then that I saw the serpent. At first, I thought that a rowboat had upturned, and my immediate response was to run to the water's edge, only to then observe the object in the water suddenly changing direction and heading off at speed, away from my position. I watched as it wriggled and churned in the water, changing direction several times before submerging beneath the waves. I waited by the shore for several minutes but of the creature I saw no further sign.

There has been tale of a creature dwelling within the loch for as far back as I can remember. However, as a respected practitioner of medicine, it would not do for me to speak of my encounter. I have spoken to no one of this matter, save for yourself. I trust that a man of your standing and expertise would be reluctant to cast aside this letter as a hoax, and implore you to visit the loch in the hope that you might report a similar experience to mine.

Yours faithfully,
Dr D. McKenzie.

Intrigued by the doctor's tale, I readied my things and hastily arranged travel to the north.

❖

Scotland welcomed me with all of her glory, or so it felt as I crossed the border, entering her lands for the first time. While England is resplendent, with her blooming meadows and rolling hills, Scotland is her rugged yet no less beautiful cousin. Hers is a terrain of jagged rock, winding roads, desolate moors and a blanket of thistle. Green and purple are her tones, and aside from the flies that nipped and buzzed about my head, this was a journey that despite taking many days to complete was one of continuous pleasant surprise.

I met the doctor at the ruins of Urquhart Castle, which, although a crumbling wreck, stood as a bold reminder of Scotland's rich and bloodied history. The ruins stand high on the banks of Loch Ness, and it was from here that we would launch our investigation come dawn.

Dr McKenzie was a curious sort, furtive and elusive. I struggled to imagine him as a trusted giver of care. Not for any concern in regard to his competence or intellect, both of which I doubted little, but more for his manner, which at times led me to feel most confounded. I assumed he might have been uncomfortable to be this near the loch, given his previous experience by the water, yet I felt a degree of disdain towards me, as though he were reluctant to be in my presence in case one of his patients should ever get wind of his association with me. Still, the doctor never said as much, nor did I ask outright. I listened as he described his encounter with the creature again, allowing him time to offer his theories, which he afforded me after considering mine. The air of unease would remain between us for the duration of the investigation.

We slept in makeshift tents hastily erected in the remains of the tower house. Though they gave us little in the way of protection from the elements, the howling gale which had whipped up with the fall of dusk faded, allowing the gentle lapping of the water upon the shoreline to usher in a sound sleep.

⁂

The next morning, I woke early so that I might observe the sun as it crept above the horizon. After a short breakfast of bread, milk and cold meats, the doctor led me down to the shore, where we walked the edge of the loch for a mile or two. Several times did he stop and point towards a bank of mud, stating that no creature known to him set aside such amounts of soil in such a way, arguing that these were places the creature had chosen to rest on the land. When questioned as to why he thought the animal would displace the earth in such a way, he countered that the mud, sodden as it was, might provide a cool place upon which to rest, and might also afford the creature a way of keeping moist away from the water.

I asked him whether he was aware of any other sightings. He spoke hurriedly of a few fishermen who, having fished these waters for generations, often told stories of a snake-like beast swimming in the loch. He went on to explain that at first he had believed the tales to have been concocted as a means of keeping away fishermen from other villages. Certainly, the stories did have this effect. By all accounts, only three boats fished the entire twenty-three-mile length of the loch.

When asked if the fishing was good, he told me that although it was possible to catch Atlantic salmon, Arctic char and pike, all species known to grow to large weights, such catches were rare, and only small examples were caught. This, he argued, was largely down to the creature that he had glimpsed; such a large animal would require a substantial amount of food were it to thrive. It was these larger fish that the beast preyed upon.

Though I could not argue against his logic, I found it hard to believe that a creature as large as the doctor had described could remain hidden from sight for so long and survive only on pike and char. True, the loch was vast. It was deemed the largest collection of inland water on the isle, and likely offered plenty of places in which a creature might hide. Still, I doubted the doctor's theory—until he showed me into the woods, that is.

I had chosen to rest by the shore. The morning's walk had been arduous, and I was hungering for lunch. A moment to sit and gather my strength while I absorbed the thoughts of the doctor seemed appealing. I sat on a large upturned piece of driftwood and glanced out across the water, wondering at what secrets it held beneath its surface.

"Mr Whyte! Come quickly, this you must see!"

The call came from the woods behind me. I stood and turned to find the doctor gesturing for me to follow. "This is what I meant earlier, come quickly!"

I picked my way across an array of rocks and assorted piles of driftwood to meet him on the forest's edge. "Come," he beckoned, before disappearing amid the tangle of trees. I followed and found him standing at the brink of a sizeable mud clearing similar to one we had observed further along the shoreline. Lying in the centre of the mound was the remains of the largest fish head I had ever seen. It had been neatly severed in half.

"Pike," offered the doctor, answering the question he knew I was about to ask. "A big one too. See how neatly it's clipped from the body?"

The pike head was as large as that of an infant. Its eye stared pitifully towards the sky.

"There's no fish in there that can do this," began Dr McKenzie. "Pike is the largest, most aggressive fish in these waters." He fixed me with an accusing look. "Now do you believe me?"

✥

In the presence of such damning evidence, it was decided that we should remain in the locale for the rest of the day. The doctor argued that, it having recently fed in the area, it seemed plausible the creature might return.

I spent the remaining hours of daylight and those early hours of nightfall sat beside the water, pensive and alert. Not once did the surface of the waters break, nor did we hear any sign of movement below. The loch remained unnaturally still, as though deliberately taunting our vigil. Weary and despondent, we pitched tents and made our camp. I recounted several stories of my work to the doctor to pass the time until the hour came to retire to our beds.

✥

The morning brought with it a chill to which I was most unaccustomed. The fields of green and purple which surrounded the loch were, on our waking, coated with frost. The forest stood tall and still, the icy winds of the north unable to stir their frozen branches. I had, of course, packed for the cold (as per my mother's warning), but my coat provided little in the way of warmth when caught in the indiscriminate blast of the wind.

The doctor, noting my discomfort, offered a dram of whiskey, saying that a stiff drink was the best defence against the unrelenting cold. Though steeped in unquestionable beauty, the Highlands were indeed an inhospitable place.

My attention was drawn to the loch, which, despite all logic, appeared to be steaming! This was a most peculiar sight and, given the conditions of our investigation, unnerved me a little as my mind raced to comprehend the forces that might be at play within the waters. The doctor, reading my concern, began to speak.

"The loch is so blasted deep that it is impossible for it to completely freeze over. Even in winds as cold as these, and I've felt colder, the surface of the loch will never freeze. Never has, never will."

I dipped my hand into the water, half-expecting it to be warm, shocked to find that it was not, and asked him how it might be possible for the water to be steaming.

"Water will freeze—you are a learned man and must agree that the laws of nature are unbreakable?"

I nodded that I agreed this was true.

"Parts of the loch do, and those parts are heavy and sink, only to be replaced by the warmer water beneath. Steam occurs when the frozen water meets with that which is warmer." Seeing the perplexed look on my face, he continued. "Fascinating sight, isn't it? Some say that the creature in the loch is from hell, and heats the water by its very presence! Some say that, but not I. I know better."

We drank our whiskey and ate our bread. The cold that had permeated my essence, having drained my muscles and caused my bones to ache, faded into the haze of my liquor-induced torpor.

"We'll take a boat today," said the doctor as he began dismantling his tent. "I know a man further down from here. He has a boat he said we could use. I didn't say what for…thought it better left between you and me. It's moored up ready for us. So long as we return it afterwards, there'll be no questions asked."

I looked out across the loch, and it suddenly dawned on me that a day on the steaming waters did not sound at all favourable.

❖

On the water and without the forest to shield us, we were at the mercy of the wind. Never before had I felt such a cold. The winds burned my flesh and made my bones ache and creak. My face was numb, the ability to talk all but lost. We took turns rowing through those steaming waters long into the night. In between lengthy bouts of silence, when my will to continue was tested most, the doctor would assure me that we stood more chance of finding the serpent if we remained on the water. I was too weary from cold to offer an alternate suggestion.

For long periods, we sat and waited. Our vessel remained steady in the calm waters. We did not drift, not even an inch. Our vision was clouded by the persistent steam; it was impossible to see anything of our surroundings beyond a few feet. Aside from sounds of the occasional flurry of fish, the loch was deathly silent.

❖

It was late at night when we first sensed the movements beneath the boat. I admit that, weary as I was, I had allowed my attention to falter and had fallen asleep. The gentle rocking of the vessel aided my slumber, and I would argue it impossible for any man to remain alert after so long an unremarkable stint spent on the water. I suspect that the doctor had likewise fallen asleep.

The movement—how best to explain? There was a sudden swell off to my left. I heard the breaking of water, a sound much louder than I had previously heard that day when shoals of fish burst free of the surface. Sitting up, I felt the motion of something large passing beneath our boat. Indeed, such was the force that our tiny vessel rose several feet from the surface of the loch before landing again with a large splash. Doctor McKenzie was so unnerved by the sudden interruption he almost fell overboard in fright, and would surely have done so had I not reached to grab him by the arm!

For several minutes, we sat in silence as the creature circled us. How do I know it was doing so? I cannot say I saw the beast, but the loud breaking of water came to us from all directions in quick succession, and several times did we feel something of great bulk brush against the sides of our boat.

On one occasion we did catch the sound of something that might resemble an animal call, the recollection of which chills me to this day. It began as a low growl, guttural and throaty, before developing into a pitched screech and ending abruptly. Though it lasted only a matter of seconds, the call echoed across the loch for several more. It was at that point that panic gripped the doctor, and he reached for the oars and began to row hard for shore. Whatever had shadowed us elected to remain behind, where the water was deep, and try as I might, I was unable to clearly observe anything of the serpent through the gloom of the night.

As the doctor rowed, the splashes of water which had surrounded our boat continued in our rear, fading in body, until barely noticeable at all.

❖

It was several days after my return home that I received the first of many letters from Doctor McKenzie. He remained adamant that we had come into close proximity with the serpent of the loch, and for several letters further continued to outline his theory that with a larger party of vigilant men, it would only be a matter of time before the beast was observed and caught. I agreed that there was something of note lurking within the waters of the loch, but as to what that might be, it was impossible to say. To conclude that the creature was a serpent rather than an as-yet-undiscovered species of fish or seal was ludicrous, given what little evidence we had gathered, though I did admit that the cry of the creature alluded to the possibility of the beast being not of fish origin.

To my knowledge, no such search was ever organised to observe and capture the monster of Loch Ness. Perhaps the doctor could find no men willing (or foolish) enough to join him on his quest, or maybe he grew tired of the chase. Whatever creature we encountered that night resides there unidentified still to this day.

Sixteen

THE INFANT VAMPYRE

Penkridge, Staffordshire, February 1874

Though I found no conclusive evidence of a serpent dwelling in Loch Ness, I thoroughly enjoyed my time in Scotland. Alas, not all investigations leave such fond memories.

I am drawn to retell the case of the infant vampyre, which, I might add, remains one of the more tragic tales I have been tasked with investigating.

I was summoned to the Staffordshire village of Penkridge by a troubled elderly woman who had spent what little in the way of savings she had amassed to secure a coach to Manchester, where she entered my father's factory and demanded that he speak with her. Upon hearing her tale, my father sent her to my door with a pocket full of coin and the promise that I might aid her woe.

As my father insisted that I aid her, I had little need for questions, at least not at this time, instead opting to arrange passage to Penkridge for the two of us. Whatever plight this woman had divulged to my father had moved him to act in spite of his own misgivings, and that alone told me urgent action was required.

As we travelled, she related the same story to me as she had told to my father. And what a tragic tale it turned out to be. Esmerelda, for that was her name, had a daughter named Abigail, who in turn had given birth to a baby boy not three weeks past. All seemed well at first. The child came into the world a healthy size and weight, and though the father was absent, Abigail, Esmerelda and her husband Peter felt duly blessed.

It soon became apparent that all was not well when the baby refused to feed. As the days passed, he became increasingly restless and weary, and no matter how many times Abigail brought him to her breast, the baby declined it.

The doctor was summoned, and after a thorough examination he concluded there was little that could be done. By now the child had lost much of its birth weight, and its skin had taken on a crimson hue. Abigail continued to attempt to feed her baby by breast, reporting that she could feel the beginnings of a tooth breaking free from his gum upon her nipple. Though a breaking tooth at such a young age is relatively unheard of, she gave it little thought, so preoccupied with worry was she.

It was only when the child bit into her breast that events took a sinister turn. The child latched onto the open wound with such fervour that, pained though Abigail was, she could not free him from her. The child, it seemed, fed upon her blood.

And he continued to do so. Each time she presented her breast to the child, he would forgo his mother's milk, opting instead to open a fresh wound and suckle on his mother's blood. The baby began to thrive, though the crimson shade of his skin continued to darken.

Word about the child's unusual feeding habit soon spread among the community, and the family began to find themselves subjected to scorn and speculation. Some had called Abigail a witch and had turned to the magistrate in the hope that he might act accordingly. Others had stoned the house and daubed it with satanic symbols.

Fearful of the growing resentment in the village and curious as to the child's feeding, Abigail had turned to her mother for help. She did not wish to lose the child to the wrath of the village, nor did she wish to hang at the whim of the magistrate. With no explanation as to why her son preferred to feed on her blood, she had no case to present to either. Fearing that it was only a matter of time before someone in the village attacked either her or her child, she tasked her mother with finding aid. Thus, having heard of my exploits in Woolpit, Esmerelda took what little money the family had set aside and travelled north in order to ask for my help.

A child and a mother in need is a plea which no man can easily ignore, and I understood why my father had sent her to my door with coin from his own pocket. He was, after all, a father too.

✥

Penkridge is a thriving market town situated in southern Staffordshire. On our arrival, the hustle that market day entailed seemed to lull as the carriage containing Esmerelda and me entered the town square. A hush fell upon the crowd of shoppers and slowly they parted to let our carriage pass through. It was immediately clear that those gathered were fearful of Esmerelda (I surmised, afraid of the unknown affliction that had cursed her offspring rather than the woman herself) and angry that the presence of her family might blight their community. The tension as we passed among their number was palpable. Countless eyes locked with mine, eyes that spoke of confusion, eyes that spoke of devout Christianity, eyes that spoke of conviction in their belief in the Lord. At that moment, I understood Esmerelda's fear and her desperate need for aid. This was a community on the brink of acting. I hurried our driver onwards.

✢

The back bedroom which housed Abigail and her infant was dark and cramped. At her bedside sat her ailing father, Peter. The child lay asleep in a cradle by the side of the bed. I introduced myself to both mother and grandfather, informing them that Esmerelda had explained the situation and that, God willing, I would find a solution to their troubles. I decided not to make known my fears regarding those I had just witnessed in the town square.

 Having received permission from the mother, I began by examining the child. Though his initial appearance disconcerted me (the skin was flushed crimson, akin to the colour of blood), the innocence of the child was clear to see. Before me lay an infant, as pure and beautiful as any born before or since. That he was afflicted with such peculiarity was far from his own fault. My mother would later say that I experienced a pang of fatherliness and that my inherent instinct to protect the vulnerable was likely raw that day like none other (at least unless I were to oneday become a father myself).

He slept soundly as I checked his torso for animal bites, his features for obvious abnormalities and his forehead to determine whether he had a high temperature. All appeared to be normal.

I turned to the mother and explained that to rule out the most absurd theories (which I wished not to discuss at this juncture for fear of frightening the family further), I would need to conduct a few simple experiments. The mother gave her permission, and I took a small mirror from my luggage.

I had read much on the subject of vampyres, and though I considered them to be a fictional creation, my work had shown me a great many wonders that I might formerly have passed off as myth. Though I believed this child to be nothing of the sort, it was good practice to rule out the impossible if one could do so.

I took the mirror and held it above the sleeping child. All in the room caught sight of his reflection. This, I assured them, was good. Then, feeling foolish (as it was apparent to me that the child was breathing), I placed the mirror close to the child's nose. Instantly the glass began to fog. I quickly removed the mirror and returned it to my bag. The mother regarded me curiously, and I for one could not blame her. Trite though my tests appeared, my duty (and my conscience) required that I carry them out in full regardless.

Next, I took a vial of holy water, uncorked it and sprinkled a couple of droplets onto the child's forehead. He stirred slightly and emitted a brief cry, but did not burst into flames or collapse as a pile of ash.

Satisfied, I explained to the mother that my experiments indicated that her child was not, at least by traditional standards, a vampyre. Addressing this unspoken fear lightened the room somewhat, the grandfather remarking that now they could take my findings to the community, so long as they could quote the words of the esteemed investigator Solomon Whyte. I assured him I would see to it that the village heard my findings directly from me.

I asked that I might speak with Abigail alone, for the issue of the child's parentage was one that needed addressing and could yield much in the way of clues as to why the infant was required to feed on human blood. Dutifully, Esmerelda and Peter obliged.

I asked her the name of the child.

"Nathaniel," she said. "After his father."

Sensing a willingness to talk of him, I asked as to his whereabouts.

"Gone, long gone," she whispered, her attention fixed upon her newborn son. "I don't know where." She explained that he had come to town with a small group of traders who were peddling wooden furniture. "It was good stuff," she said with a smile. "Small stools and such, nicely crafted." The two of them had begun a conversation which continued long into the night. She admitted that she was taken by his polite and gentlemanly manner and that when he made a move to kiss her, she invited him to continue. They made love that night, and at the height of his arousal, he bit hard into her neck, drawing blood. She described the pain of the bite as overwhelming, yet somehow it entangled itself in her throes of pleasure. He suckled at her neck as he planted his seed inside her, before retreating into the night, never to be seen again.

As she recounted her story, the evident love that she felt for the man carried lightly in the tone of her voice. When she showed me the scars that blemished the pure white flesh of her neck, not once did she appear shamed. For a time, I wondered if she ought, before deciding not. This was an experience which, although fleeting, had brought her the greatest gift of all, a child of her own. The circumstance of its conception was, of course, unusual, at least in the eyes of you and me, but to Abigail, that was likely the most memorable and sacred night of her young life. Who was I to judge her?

I thanked her for sharing this information and informed her that I would check in to the local coach house for the evening to study my notes, before returning in the morning to offer my conclusions. She seemed content with this, and I left when Nathaniel woke, so that he might feed in peace.

❖

I spent that evening in the privacy of my room, far from the racket of the bustling bar, poring over the collection of books I had packed before hurriedly leaving for Penkridge. My investigations all pointed towards the theory that the father might indeed be the reason the child needed to feed on blood. Folklore describes a condition whereby afflicted individuals are required to drink fresh blood on an almost daily basis. To many, this is known as vampyrism. That these people are said to be of vampyre origin is, of course, no surprise. However, regarding the traditional view, they are as far removed from the monsters of folklore as you and I. They are not undead, cannot manifest themselves as bats or mists and are not afraid of holy water. For reasons unknown (though many scholars believe it is a matter of mind rather than body), afflicted individuals are required to sustain themselves on a diet of blood. Having heard Abigail's testimony with regard to the conception of the child and his apparent need to feed on blood, I had to conclude that whatever the ailment, in this case, it had passed from father to son.

Though not a conclusion to fill one's spirit with hope, for I could find no mention of a cure, I comforted myself with the knowledge that by sharing my findings with the family and then the community at large, I might be able to dispel a large portion of the fear which had gripped the community and afford the family a life of relative peace. As I settled myself to sleep, I had no idea just how wrong I was.

✧

I awoke to shouts of panic and the acrid stench of smoke. At first, I thought the coach house was alight, and I leapt from my bed to the nearest window. Throwing aside the curtains, I caught sight of a house further towards the edge of town aflame. The streets nearby were filled with people shouting. None seemed to be attempting to douse the fire. It was then that I realised the house that was alight was the same one I had visited earlier that day.

✧

I fought through the chaotic crowd that had gathered at the scene of the fire. Most were angry, yelling taunts and insults that were lost against the roar of the flames. Some directed their hate towards a small group huddled at the side of the road opposite the burning building. Abigail and her mother and father sat with their backs to the crowd, huddled in a circle. I pushed through the rabble and reached for them, placing my hand on Peter's shoulder. Startled, he whirled upon me, eyes red with fury, tears staining his cheeks. Recognising me and sensing no threat, he turned back towards the bundle of cloth which he and his family sat around. The townsfolk continued to shout and jeer. Choking on the stifling smoke, I leaned in closer to see what lay in the pile of tattered cloth, only to draw back in horror when I realised it was the body of baby Nathaniel. A tiny wooden stake pierced his chest.

I fell to my knees, overcome with remorse, furious with the mob for opting to murder. As the four of us wept together, the remains of their home continued to burn.

⸙

I elected to remain in the town for the funeral. Few outside of the family attended. The community had been gripped by a sense of silent brooding since the events of that fateful night. It was not only the family who wished to see the infant interred in the ground; the townsfolk too wanted to confine their darkest hour to history. Burying the child would more easily allow them to forget their deeds.

The priest refused to let Nathaniel be buried in the usual grounds of the cemetery, insisting that it was not for reason of superstition or folklore (he stated to me several times that he did not believe the child to be a vampyre or an advocate of Satan) but one of doctrine. Nathaniel, it transpired, had not been baptised. Therefore, the only plot he could occupy must fall within the north side of the cemetery.

The family could not afford a headstone, having spent their savings on the journey to request my aid. I purchased one on their behalf. Again, I ran into opposition from the church. They would not allow us to add the name of the child to the stone.

The body of Nathaniel lies in Penkridge Cemetery. It is marked with a headstone bearing a skull and crossbones. I visit it every year to commemorate the anniversary of his burial.

Seventeen

AFTERMATH

The loss of the child affected me profoundly. Even now, all these years later, the feelings of woe weigh heavily upon me. Grief brings with it wounds that will not heal. The same pain, the same crushing sorrow, is felt now as was then. Nathaniel was murdered where he lay, and I held myself responsible. Not for the first time (nor the last), I concluded that life was a journey centred around the concept of loss.

Fate chose not to bless me with a child of my own, and often I wonder whether the path I opted to follow might have had some bearing on that. Nathaniel was the only charge granted my protection, and I failed him. I often question whether this was a test of sorts, to see if my character could withstand the pressures of fatherhood. Fate presented me with the protection of an innocent, whose family trusted me to make the correct decisions regarding his well-being. If it was a test, then I failed it miserably. Not a day passes that I do not think of him. Often I imagine what kind of man he would have become. Judging by the short time I spent with his family, I would wager a fine one.

Countless times I have lamented my decision to delay deliverance of my conclusion to the family and people of the town until morning. Had I returned to Abigail that evening, chances are I would have been present when the crowd, afraid and confused, forced their way into Nathaniel's quarters. Might I have been able to reason with them in spite of their fear? I cannot say for sure. I know, however, that I would have been better placed to intercept the murderous swine who drove the stake into the defenceless child's heart. I'd have given my life for the boy, of that I am certain.

Whenever I am reminded of that fateful night, a rage unbecoming of me takes hold. This was a family who, through no fault of their own, suffered immeasurably at the hands of ignorance. This was a child whose life was taken by those blinded by religion and their own lack of foresight. Had they held a degree of civility until dawn, I might have been able to instil reason into their minds.

I have seen similar events occur several times during my work. Where communities, gripped by fear and fuelled by the proclamations of the self-righteous, take arms and commit atrocities in the name of God. Many are the perpetrators, yet few are those willing to accept their sin. Each time I have held myself accountable. How could I not? Having inserted myself into the fervour that grips such a community, an outsider seeking to introduce a sense of logic and reason so that all concerned might sleep soundly in their beds once more! Surely I ought to be able to prevent such tragedy? Surely the failure is mine?

Many times I have quarrelled with myself over this very question. My sense of duty argues that, as a sound and learned man, yes, I ought to be able to steer the ignorant, the fearful and the misguided away from actions that would later be deemed abhorrent. However, there is the side of me which, as experience has taught, rationalises that the human condition is often such that in times of duress, it cannot be checked. When gripped by a mood of fear and confusion, it is rarely possible to predict how one individual might react compared to the next. This is further compounded when scores of similarly afflicted people congregate. Mob rule is oft unpredictable and savage.

I needed to accept that I cannot affect the way people think and the most I can do is offer an answer that might at best placate them. This was not the case at Woolpit, where my conclusions incited further fear. Nor was this the case at Penkridge, where I left it too late to deliver my verdict. At Blakemere, despite my warnings, Stranfold turned up dead, a possible victim of the mermaid I had so warned him of!

In these cases, it is impossible to say whether I could have saved the lives that were lost. I see that now, although it took many years for me to accept it. I did what I could, and sometimes that would never be enough. I have made mistakes too, mistakes that I must take to my grave, and I do so willingly—now, at least. Not always, but now. There are many more examples of such, but they shall keep for another day.

✣

For weeks after the incident at Penkridge, I was disconsolate. I barely ate nor drank. Night bled into day and day into night as I remained at my desk, lost in thought, a plethora of notes scattered before me. Thoughts turned to Jasmine, and though I had heard little from her, my heart lifted slightly at her memory. With no one else in whom I could confide, I penned a letter to her in which I laid bare the events that had led to baby Nathaniel's passing and my own thoughts upon the matter.

The writing lifted the burden of my woe a little. I found the simple act of documenting my pain highly cathartic. I admit now that I wept many times during the composition of that letter.

With it complete, I was caught in two minds as to whether to send it. I wished not to burden her with my grief, yet felt that whatever connection we shared meant she might not only be able to understand my pain, but to alleviate it, if only a little.

Her reply is detailed in full below. I read it often.

My dear Solomon,

Thank you for writing. I shall hate to think of you suffering alone.

Please allow me to spend little time exchanging pleasantries, as I know that is not the reason that you wrote me.

I am in good health, and all is well here at the house. Again you ask, and again I shall answer, the skull remains silent. I believe that the action taken was deemed satisfactory, for truly the house is blessed with a presence of calm.

The Lord ails fairly; his health, though not in any feeble state, is falling short of what I am accustomed to. The maids attend to his every need and I, as his lady wife, do what is required.

Though I ought not speak of this, yes, I find thoughts of you enter my head entirely of their own fancy. I am sure you understand the reason why I choose not to dwell upon these, for my place is here.

Now, to matters concerning you. I am heartbroken to hear the fate of poor Nathaniel, but promise me this: you must accept no fault as your own! You are a man of kind heart, wishing only to help those in need. How were you to foresee the actions that would unfold that night? It is inhuman! To anticipate such deeds is to turn one's back upon humanity itself, and I know that is not in your character to do.

You must not punish yourself for the evil deeds of others. Many times, your work (should you choose to persevere) shall place you into situations where fear, anger and hate abound. Stay true to your heart, for yours carries the wish to help, to alleviate such feelings and to explain the cause behind the chaos. Many people have benefitted from your intervention already, and more shall do so.

Stay the path, for it is yours to tread.

Sincerely,

Jasmine

X

Eighteen

THE SLEEPING SAVIOUR

Choosing to ignore the requests that lay piled on my desk, I turned instead to my collection of books detailing Britain's folklore for my next investigation. Distraction was required, for the events of Penkridge haunted me still. I was in no mindset to task myself with a study where the choices I made might involve unseen misery and consequence for those the case concerned. Instead, I opted to try to uncover the truth behind one of our isle's favourite sons: Arthur Pendragon.

There is much debate as to whether the legendary king did, in fact, exist at all. Though there are countless tales telling of his exploits, many are contradictory, and it is commonly believed that Arthur was nothing more than a fictional creation. Whether King Arthur reigned over

Britain during the fifth and sixth centuries AD or not, his legacy remains, and his heroic exploits provide the foundations for an array of stories that, despite their questionable origin, have been spoken of for generations.

My interest in Arthur's legend concerns his final resting place, for which three possibilities are most commonly talked about. These are Glastonbury Tor, Alderley Edge and Cadbury Castle. It was my intention to explore all three locations in the hope that I might uncover the truth behind our country's greatest monarch, once and for all.

❖

Alderley Edge.
Cheshire, July 1874

Of the three possible burial grounds, Alderley Edge lay closest to Manchester. It is a tiny hamlet, not fifteen miles from my home. Common sense dictated that I explore the nearby caves associated with Arthurian legend first, before embarking south to Somerset once I had ruled out Alderley Edge as Arthur's final resting place.

You may ask why such a desolate and secluded maze of caverns might be associated with the legend of Arthur. Were it not for the existence of a spring, the water of which trickles out from the rocks beneath the visage of an elderly man that some deem to be an impression of Merlin (the fabled wizard of Arthur's court), there would be scant reason to suspect that Arthur had ever visited the area. The village is surrounded by thick forest, untold numbers of caverns and craggy rock formations, all of which add further character to the assorted tales of Arthur that the area claims as its own.

A farmhand showed me into the forest, talking excitedly of the miscellaneous sprites and boggarts that were said to call her home. I listened with only a passing interest, as many of the tales recounted were slight alterations of ones I had heard many times over. Still, it would not have been polite to dampen his enthusiasm, and I played the part of the active listener.

After an hour or so we emerged into a clearing, where before us stood a towering wall of rock. A faint trickle of water could be heard above the ambiance of the forest, though I was forced to examine the rocks carefully to be able to ascertain where the sound came from, so weak was the flow.

Having located the source of the spring, I traced the water until I spied what many had claimed to be the carving of Merlin's face. In such a light as the summer day afforded, I agree that at a particular angle and when it was cast in particular shadow, one might interpret the shape of the rock to resemble that of a face. To my eyes, I saw the resemblance as a mere trick of the light and the rock formation as nothing more than a natural occurrence. There had been mention of an inscription located beneath the carving in several of my books. Of this, I found no sign.

My guide thought otherwise, and when I asked as to just how he imagined someone might be able to carve the image of an elderly gentleman halfway up what I accounted to be a sheer rock face, he merely replied that the carver had climbed. I chose not to argue with his logic. The farmhand, who was no more than thirteen, continued with his theory, citing that Merlin watched over the final resting place of Arthur from high atop those rocks so that he might sleep soundly until the day arrived when England required his aid once more. A romantic tale for sure, though I couldn't help but wonder what might qualify as England's need. After all, Arthur had remained absent during the Norman Invasion. Nor had he been present during the outbreak of the Black Death or the early fires which blighted London.

Unperturbed, I followed in the eager footsteps of my youthful guide until we reached the entrance to a series of caverns. This, he proclaimed, was the final resting place of not only Arthur but his company of knights. According to him, they lay undiscovered in the deeper reaches of the caverns. When pressed as to why no one had thought to explore and chart said caverns, the boy claimed that none had dared to out of respect.

Now a seasoned cavern explorer (or so I foolishly believed), I elected to enter alone. I carried with me a large ball of fine yet robust fishing line. I trusted one end to the boy, instructing him that no matter how long I was absent, he was not to let go of the line, as this would be the means through which I would find my way out of the caverns. He nodded meekly, and I saw the fear of responsibility take hold of him, his face quickly draining of all colour. With the fate of a quick retreat resting solely in the hands of the young boy, I withdrew my pocket tinderbox and entered the mouth of the cave.

Familiar sounds and smells flooded my senses, and suddenly I felt instantly transported back to the time I had spent underground in Woolpit. The mind has a peculiar knack for recalling memories as if they had taken place yesterday, particularly if scent plays a role in such memories. The air inside the caves was cold and laden with moisture, but the aroma of the earth seemed sweet. The trip through the caverns of Alderley Edge, though not altogether pleasant, certainly did much to dismiss the memories of the fetid passageways that littered the area surrounding Woolpit.

Several hours were spent underground, and not one anomaly did I find. Beyond this, I sensed no tangible feeling of there being *more* in the air. How best to explain, as likely at this point I sound vague?

As my experience in the field of paranormal investigation grew, I became aware that I harboured a latent sense that only made its presence felt when there was something amiss that I had previously overlooked. This sense developed over the years, and one could say it might have been a heightened form of intuition. Had I dedicated time to study it further, I might have a more profound explanation as to its origin and purpose.

However, I ramble. My intuition proved correct. I emerged from the caverns later that evening having found nothing of note. The farmhand had remained as he had promised he would, the line still held in his hand. Alderley Edge, pleasant though the visit was, yielded little in the way to convince me that Arthur Pendragon lay buried within her lands. Thankful for an afternoon well spent, I turned my attentions to the south.

✣

Glastonbury Tor.
Glastonbury, Somerset, August 1874

Glastonbury Tor has an array of myths and legends attached to the site, not least that some believe Joseph of Aramathea came to this place preaching the Gospel, bringing with him the Cup of Christ (more commonly known as the Holy Grail). It is also said that he founded the abbey that now lies broken and derelict nearby, thus immortalising Glastonbury as the first Christian site in the country. Many believe the Grail to be buried beneath the third and largest tor (The tors are a series of hills that stand tall amidst the lowlands of Somerset. Their exact origin is unknown).

However, my concern was not with the religious connection to the tors, but the tales that tie the site to the mythos of Arthur. Long ago, it was believed that the tors were surrounded by water, making them islands, the largest of which was named Avalon. Avalon featured heavily in Arthur's legend. It was the place where his sword Excalibur was forged, and it was where his wounded body was ferried after the Battle of Camlann, or so the stories say. Should the tor indeed be the fabled isle of Avalon, I concluded that I might find clues as to Arthur's burial place somewhere within its grounds.

The tor is a magical place by day. Dominating the skyline, it rises like a beacon, atop it sitting the crumbling tower of St Michael's Church. Whether Arthur lies here or not, the site is integral to a great many religious beliefs and provides the backdrop for dozens of tales.

This was a place I explored in solitude. Again, I felt no presence or dark intent, only the air of calm that lingers in the most sacred of sites. I believed that the tor had tales to tell, I was just uncertain as to whether Arthur featured among them. Even should the legend prove to be a work of fiction, I could only imagine the inspiring site the tors once would have been when surrounded by water. Such an image would no doubt have fired countless imaginations! There was magic here: the magic of storytelling.

I spent several hours examining the symbols that adorned the remains of the church and the abbey, yet could find nothing which might relate to the tale of Arthur. My books had discussed the previous unearthing of a pair of skeletal remains in 11 AD, which many believed to be the bones of Arthur and Lady Guinevere. The argument was thus: the tors acted as burial mounds, and King Henry II (who was attempting to stave off a Welsh uprising) uncovered the bodies in the hope that it might mean an end to the Welsh hopes of their king returning from death to aid them. I had seen similar (but smaller mounds) elsewhere in the country, and though it was later reported that the skeletons had been placed in order to be *found* by King Henry and his men, many still believed that Arthur lay buried deep within one of the tors.

The tors seemed a possible resting site, that I could not argue against, but I felt that there would be a marker or a symbol hidden somewhere that would allude to this. I found nothing that might be interpreted as such. So, with neither the means, permission nor willpower to dig into the hearts of the tors, I elected to resume my search for Arthur at the site of nearby Cadbury Castle.

❖

Cadbury Castle.
South Cadbury, Somerset, August 1874

Here was a place I would describe as having a certain *magical* feeling in the air. Perhaps in my gut, I always suspected that this site more than the others might hold the key to the truth behind Arthur and his place of burial. Indeed, the castle was known as Camlet for many centuries. Legend either dwelt within the walls that once stood upon this vast mound, or inspired them.

Lying only eleven miles south of Glastonbury Tor, a stronghold has stood on this site since the Iron Age. Built high atop the surrounding lowlands, the fortress was afforded expansive views on all sides.

There remains nothing of the castle that once dominated the Somerset skyline, which gave me little hope of finding any evidence of Arthur's legacy. At first glance, there is only sculpted land and forest. No stone or mortar survives this place and has not for many centuries. Still, by reading the lie of the land, one can easily imagine how the structure once stood.

I walked the folds of earth that surrounded the base of the hill. I walked the ramparts, and I walked the forests. I walked them with diligence. There was the feeling that something lay hidden here. Again, I cannot describe it other than to say I knew that there was more to this site than met the eye. This was a place of great significance.

Day melted into night but still I walked until, quite by accident, the heel of my boot caught on something metallic and unseen. I shall not say where and you shall understand why in due course.

I searched the grass at my feet, pulling great tufts free from the earth until the glint of metal caught in moonlight drew my attention. I dug with my fingers, gradually uncovering a small iron ring. Grasping the ring with my thumb and forefinger, I pulled, not with any degree of force (for I hardly expected anything to occur—I saw the ring and instinct said *pull*), and to my surprise, the earth before me lifted with ease.

The trapdoor appeared to be made of stone, yet I had lifted it with but one finger! The mud and soil upon it remained unspoiled and for a moment I sat, toying with the weight of the thing, which, and I cannot for the life of me begin to explain it, appeared to be nothing at all. Below was a stone staircase which descended into darkness. I set the trapdoor aside, removed my hydrogen lighter from my pocket and followed the steps down into the bowels of the earth.

I counted thirty-three steps before I reached level ground. Before me lay a stone-cut arched chamber which curved gently to my left before disappearing out of sight. Periodically, lanterns hung from the walls, their flames burning blue. I returned my lighter to my pocket, for the torches provided ample light. I passed close by the first and felt no lick of heat from the flame. I moved my hand over it and felt nothing. How they burnt I cannot say. It was evident to me that this was a place in which few had ever trodden.

I continued along the length of the passageway for several minutes. As I travelled deeper, the curve of the tunnel seemed to tighten, as though I were walking in an ever-decreasing circle. The features of the passage never altered.

Eventually, I emerged into an antechamber, where a pair of gilded doors blocked my way. Inscribed upon them were numerous symbols and designs, some of which were instantly familiar (I had seen similar designs in many texts). My pulse quickened as I pushed them open and stumbled into an ornate throne room.

The room featured walls that were impossibly high, for where I saw a ceiling, there ought to have been the clear Somerset night sky. The walls were lined with tapestries that told tales of legendary battles, each involving the Knight King and his sword of legend.

There were three thrones set at the far end of the hall. The one to the left held the slumped skeletal remains of the man I took to be king; such was the size of the crown fastened upon his head and the ornate design of the sword which lay upon his knees. To his right sat another, wearing a slight yet elegant tiara and a flowing gown of golden thread. Between them sat a third throne. The occupant of this was a child, probably no more than the age of five or six upon death. Fastened on the skull was a small tiara.

✥

Leaving that place, I felt a fresh sense of vigour. I had discovered the final resting place of King Arthur and his queen. Not only had I found proof that the king of legend had in fact existed, but I had also found evidence of his lineage that the tales had previously ignored. Arthur had sired a daughter.

Recalling this story now, I am torn as to whether to divulge the exact location of Arthur's tomb. I know that none have visited since, for I doubt that anyone could keep such a discovery as much of a secret as I. Discovering that myth is actually fact returned to me the sense of adventure I had previously lost as a result of recent experiences. I realised that not all of my investigations would end in tragedy and that I might, in fact, better the lives of many through my work.

I have kept the discovery of Arthur's resting place to myself for decades. This was selfish of me I know, yet every time I wavered in my self-belief, every time I questioned my work's worth, I would think back to that summer's night spent at Cadbury Castle and smile. I kept my find secret so that I might draw strength from the memory when doubt threatened most. Finding Arthur and his family was my private achievement, proof that there is magic and more in the world. Needing this no longer, I shall share the location of the trapdoor which leads to King Arthur's tomb.

South-eastern ramparts (outer reach). Two trees grow alone together, almost entirely parallel to one another. The trapdoor lies between them. Dig for the ring.

Be respectful upon gracing the king and his family with your presence.

Nineteen
THE FALLEN HOUSE

Hales Hall, Cheadle, Staffordshire, September 1874

Upon my return to usual duties, the first letter that caught my interest came from a Mr Cecil Plant, who, having been tasked by the bank to sell Hales Hall, an eighteenth-century manor house located in the quiet town of Cheadle, Staffordshire, had written to seek my aid on the matter. While he wrote little as to the nature of his problem, he explained that only a person with my background and knowledge would be able to both understand the essence of his dilemma and offer a possible solution.

❖

I met Mr Plant at the entrance to the property. He was a small man of smart appearance, though the shadows beneath his eyes and the puffiness in his cheeks suggested that the stresses of his duties were beginning to take a toll on him. We exchanged pleasantries, and he showed me inside, marching ahead and insisting that we get "*straight to it.*"

We passed numerous rooms, all of which were devoid of furniture and character. The building seemed to house an oppressive atmosphere, one I took to be due to the lack of occupation and the general state of disrepair. Mr Plant chatted all during our brief passage through the house, explaining how the previous owner, Dr Raymond Chartstess, had fallen upon hard times, having lost his wife, his silk mill and eventually the ownership of the hall.

Reaching the doors to the study, Mr Plant paused for a moment. "Prepare yourself for quite the oddest sight that you might ever see!" he warned, before throwing open the door. "Behold, see what remains of the former owner." He pointed to a spot in the centre of the room. "Try as we might, we cannot rid this place of his stain."

The study was bare save for a thick scarlet carpet. Blood spattered the white of the ceiling at irregular intervals, and a pool had collected in the centre of the carpet. The scent of iron hung heavy in the air and the atmosphere of the room at once began to both sing and scream. My head started to spin and I felt suddenly nauseous. I reached for the frame of the door to steady myself for a moment.

"Quite the sight, isn't it?" remarked Mr Plant. "Would you believe that this is the third carpet we've laid? All at the bank's expense, might I add. But who would want to buy a property still covered in the blood of its former owner, I ask? Would you?"

I shook my head and regained my composure. The atmosphere of the room was a heady mix of torment and anguish: exposure to it had affected me in a way I had not expected. Mr Plant, however, seemed oblivious to both the character of the room and its effect upon me. I did not know it then, but this was a sign that I was becoming more attuned to the supernatural. My third eye and my intuition were gradually becoming one and the same.

"Go on, touch it," said Mr Plant. "You'll find it wet. Always is. No matter how many carpets we lay, no matter how many times the poor maids scrub it away, it keeps seeping back through. Same as the stain on the ceiling. Look." He pointed towards the spattered pattern of blood. "Sometimes it drips if we leave it for too long." He puckered his face in disgust. "Most unpleasant."

I asked him how the blood had come to stain the ceiling.

"Arterial spray. Or so the physician said when I asked the same. I wouldn't know. Never seen a dead one before."

Tentatively, my head still spinning, I entered the room. The feelings of despair that the room contained increased with every step I took towards the dark puddle on the carpet. Swallowing hard and focusing my concentration, I bent towards the stain and brushed my fingers over the surface. They came away thick with blood. I tasted my fingertips to ascertain whether the substance was indeed what it appeared to be. From the corner of my eye, I saw Mr Plant grimace.

I asked him if this was a hoax, citing that if it were, it was a humourless joke to play, such was the amount of fresh blood splashed onto the carpet and ceiling. He assured me that it was not. The property was securely locked on leaving each night, remaining so until he arrived the next morning. Regardless of how many hours the maids spent scrubbing the stain away, come the reopening of the study the next day, the stains were back, fresh and wet.

With the noise of the room in my head beginning to subside, I asked as to the fate of Dr Chartstess.

"Sad, really, but a sign of the times. His silk mill down Brookhouse way went belly up. He couldn't compete with the new factories that have sprung up of late. When the money dried up, his wife took off. Not sure where. She didn't show up for the funeral. With her gone, he was alone with his debt. I know he didn't want to give up the hall, it had been in his family for generations, you see… but the bank needs its debts paid…and well, they had to take it in the end. People say that he was so overcome with grief he took a razor to his throat, and well…you've seen the mess. This was five weeks ago now…I'm at a loss to explain what is going on, and as you can imagine, no one wants to buy a house covered in blood!"

I nodded, joining Mr Plant in the study doorway, the noise in my head diminishing further with every step towards the exit.

"Do you know what might be causing this?" he asked, a hopeful look on his face.

I shook my head and instructed that the maids be sent for so that I might observe their efforts to clear away the blood. Once satisfied, I said, I would ensure that all doors and windows that provided access to the room were nailed shut. I then suggested I spend the night keeping vigil. Relieved that I had taken his issue seriously, he dutifully agreed and set off to find the hall's cleaning employees.

❖

The maids worked tirelessly throughout the afternoon, preparing the study to my exact instruction. I decided that it would prove futile to clean the carpet at this point—its presence only hindered my investigation—so I ordered it stripped back so that the floor beneath be exposed. The polished oak floorboards were stained far more than the carpet above might suggest, and the maids worked until all traces of blood were removed. A similar effort was applied to the spatter on the ceiling, though as this was a much smaller, less concentrated amount of blood, this was removed quickly. Content with their efforts, I set about sealing the windows. At first, Mr Plant objected to my methods, citing that it would incur a great cost to replace and repair the damage done by my meddling, but after explaining the importance of setting a controlled environment, one that I knew to be all but impossible to enter without my knowledge, he relented.

Come dusk, I bid farewell to Mr Plant and his cleaning staff, assuring him that by morning I would endeavour to provide him with answers. Reluctantly, he retired home.

✥

Exposed to the atmosphere of the house alone, I was able to better get a feel for the place. Here was a hall that, while grand and opulent at one time, had fallen into a state of disrepair, a result of unforeseen bad luck. There was no impression of *home* here, only an oppressive sense of brooding and remorse. With my back rested against the wall of the study, I pulled my blanket tightly to my chest and wished for dawn.

✥

It was after midnight when I heard what at first I interpreted to be distant but definite groans. Several times did I walk the floors of the hall to locate their origin. Each time I returned to my vigil outside of the study none the wiser as to their origin. My weary mind argued that it might be nothing more than a result of the howling gale which had buffeted the walls and windows of the hall for several hours.

Suddenly I caught the sound of an anguished voice emanating from within the study. The voice was male, the tone fearful and aggrieved. With time neither for thought nor reason, I took to the door with my hammer, clawing at the nails which I had used earlier to seal the door closed. As I did so, the voice in the study grew louder. I worked quickly, for whoever was inside was likely responsible for the bloodstains and was mere seconds from apprehension.

The final nail gave way. I forced the door open and stumbled inside, where I caught sight of an elderly gentleman, garbed in black silk trousers and a white shirt, taking a razor-blade to his throat and with one fluid motion slicing it open. Gushes of blood arced upwards, spattering and staining the pristine white ceiling, and a ragged scream of anguish filled the air. Panic took hold of me, and I moved towards the man so that I might aid him, only to watch in disbelief as he fell to the floor and vanished before my eyes. All that remained in the study was a rapidly expanding puddle of blood and the echoing cries of Dr Chartstess.

✣

It was dawn when Mr Plant discovered me sitting outside the open study. My face was speckled with blood, as were my clothes. I dare not imagine what his first thought upon catching sight of me might have been, but from the look of terror on his face, I fear he thought I had committed murder in his absence.

Ignoring me, he rushed into the study, mouth agape, before proclaiming, "It's bloody back again! I knew it, I bloody knew it!" I joined him at the puddle of blood and explained what I had witnessed earlier that morning.

❖

"So you are saying that you saw his ghost?" said Mr Plant, blinking profusely as he tried to comprehend my words.

I nodded and suggested that the local parish priest might be the most appropriate person with whom to speak regarding the matter. My studies had included several cases where blessings had been administered unto a property or object, and while I did not fully understand the science behind the ritual, I knew well enough that I was fully incapable of conducting one successfully.

I left Mr Plant and his team of housemaids as they worked to remove the stain from the floor.

❖

Later that year I received a further letter from Mr Plant, thanking me for my time and informing me of the action chosen by the bank. Apparently a blessing had been carried out by a priest from a neighbouring parish, albeit unsuccessfully. Mr Plant assured me that the blood stains still remained and that he had passed the task of the hall's sale on to a colleague.

To my knowledge, Hales Hall stands vacant and unsold.

Twenty

THE BELLS OF WEREDALE

Wastwater, Wasdale, Cumbria, July 1875

A university professor by the name of Harold Bromby had written to me during the autumn of 1874 to inform me of a tale from his childhood. Professor Bromby explained how he had lived in Cumbria, near to the body of water known locally as Wastwater, where the story of the fictional village of Weredale was often spoken of. Weredale, it was said, had been a tiny hamlet once situated on the banks of Wastwater. The story tells that there was a particular summer entirely devoid of sun, one where it rained constantly for a month. The lake, unaccustomed to such heavy rainfall, began to swell until its banks struggled to contain its waters. One night in July, while the village slept, the lake burst its banks.

Within minutes, the hamlet was submerged, and it is said that not one villager escaped the flood. Those near to the shores of the lake during the month of July often tell of the tolling of an unseen bell, emanating from beneath the surface. Professor Bromby offered that this might be a toll of warning, perhaps similar to one uttered by a vigilant soul who, having seen the oncoming flood, scaled the steps of the church steeple and rang the bell in a bid to warn those still sleeping of impending peril. It is said that on a particularly dry summer's day, the spire of Weredale church can be seen protruding from the waters.

The professor asked that I explore the area come July, with the intention of reporting my findings to him and his students the following autumn. Intrigued by the story, I wrote to Jasmine, inviting her to join me on the banks of Wastwater for what promised to be a curious (and more importantly, safe) night of investigation. On the morning of my departure some several months later, I had yet to receive a reply.

❖

I opted to alight at Santon Bridge, which was the nearest village to the lake. The weather being pleasant, I decided not to secure a room at the local tavern, instead choosing to pitch a tent lakeside. This would afford me ample time to investigate the lake without needing to cut short my visit to hike back to the village.

Wastwater was a sight to behold. Though nowhere near as expansive as Loch Ness, she was every bit as picturesque. Flanked by mountains on either side and bookended by craggy flatlands, the water lay still and undisturbed, mirroring the cloudless summer sky with perfect symmetry. The winds that I had expected to thunder between the mountains and across the flatlands were noticeable in their absence. Indeed, this was a pleasant place in which to spend a summer's eve.

I pitched my tent at the lake's edge, choosing a location that afforded me a vast, uninterrupted view of the water. That day was one of the warmest in recent times, if memory serves correctly, though no sign of the Weredale Parish steeple could I see.

I spent several hours walking the banks, determining in my mind where the lake of old had lain before the flood, and where Weredale might lie beneath the surface. It is important to mention that a village by the name of Werdell was mentioned in the Domesday Book, and was described as being located ashore a vast expanse of water in this area. The last mention of Weredale occurred in 1724, courtesy of an explorer's guide to the area. Henry Covill's *Foothills and the Lakes* contained accounts and maps of the area. He described Weredale as *a charming yet naïve backwater, rife with rose-cheeked parlour maids and grubby little children*. He estimated the population as sixty-three. I also found reference to a series of floods that blighted the area in 1672, though there was nothing at all of the fate of Weredale. History books make no mention of the village, save for those references noted above.

I returned to my tent at the onset of dusk. My limbs ached and my spirit, though weary, was content. There were worse places to spend the night, I reasoned, and with the clear sky slowly beginning to darken, I kindled a small fire and watched the stars wake.

❖

I caught her scent, sweet and light, long before I heard her place her luggage onto the ground behind me. The sense of smell is often largely overlooked, but I have found it to be quite capable of instantly conjuring memories with an astounding depth of clarity. Jasmine's perfume had just such an effect upon me, and for a moment, I was lost in memories of our embrace at Mersea's cemetery.

I waited, curious as to what she might do next. After a while of listening to her rummaging and rustling, I stood and turned to face her. Jasmine had busied herself erecting a tent of her own. She paused for a moment, smiled, then asked if I had given much thought to the helping of a lady in need.

✥

Having eaten, we warmed ourselves by the fire I had lit earlier that evening. I regaled her with the story of Weredale, and she, with high interest, asked for my opinion of the tale. I explained my doubts as to the village's existence, and she listened attentively. Having seemingly heard enough, she nodded and remarked that I was still as cynical as the day we had first met. I nodded and laughed. After a moment of awkward silence, both of our attentions returned to the water, the surface of which reflected the night sky in all of her glory. Such was the stillness of the water, the urge was great that we should cast aside our cares (and our clothes) and wade headlong into the heavens.

✥

"I loved him, you know. Once, anyway." It was Jasmine who broke the expectant silence. "He was once so driven, so confident. It was never about his money; you understand that, I'm sure?"

I nodded. I saw Jasmine's soul, or so I believed, though I would not say as much at the time. Greed played no part in her character.

"It was always the man behind the title who fascinated me," she continued. "Few ever saw his spirit. They only ever met a practised, refined man, a diligent man playing a role. Perhaps that is what is killing him."

I turned to her, unsure as to how I might comfort her. Her eyes remained locked on the surface of the water, and I decided it would be better to let her talk.

"He has not long for this world, of that I am sure. The physicians are at a loss as to what ails him. I have given my all in terms of care and attention, but when you sent your invitation, try as I might to ignore all thought of seeing you again, I could not. I am here for respite. I am here because I feel at one with you, though I ought not to. What happened in Mersea—"

I interrupted, saying that no explanation was needed and that I would gladly relieve her of whatever burdens weighed upon her soul. She smiled at me, and I placed my arm around her shoulders. She rested her head on my chest, and her posture eased as she relaxed onto me. At that moment, I felt complete.

✤

We woke with a start. The noise that filled the air seemed extraordinary yet strangely familiar. Still feeling the effects of a rapidly retreating slumber, we climbed to our feet. The noise was coming from the lake.

We stood in silence for several moments, neither of us daring to speak for fear of breaking the other's concentration. The sound had a steady rhythm. Its tone rose and fell in regular increments.

"Bells!" said Jasmine, her eyes alive with excitement. "It sounds like church bells!"

At that moment, as though by invitation, the tolling of the bells (and I have no idea how this was possible) burst free from the distortion of the water, ringing loud and clear across the valley. Such was the noise that Jasmine and I covered our ears to protect them!

The pealing of bells was quickly joined by another sound, a sound at first distant that built quickly in fury and intensity, eventually drowning out the sound of the bells altogether. Jasmine turned to me, a look of concern on her face.

The roar of oncoming water rose to an almost inaudible din. Afraid, Jasmine grabbed ahold of me and I her. My senses were in conflict. On the one hand, my hearing told me that a wall of water was rapidly surging towards us, yet my eyes relayed only images of calm.

The rush of unseen water washed over us before finally beginning to recede. Jasmine trembled as I held her and whispered soothing sentiment in a bid to calm her nerves. After a moment more the sound of the water had subsided completely, and all was silent once again.

Having collected herself, Jasmine released her grip on me and took a step back. "The water? You heard it? I'm sure you did. Where did it go?"

I nodded and was about to offer an explanation when I caught sight of a luminous trail of light weaving beneath the surface of the water. Jasmine noted the direction of my gaze (and no doubt my look of surprise) and turned towards the water.

Where a breath before there had been a single trail of light beneath the water, there were suddenly many. Jasmine and I watched in awe as within moments the entire lake was bathed in an effervescent aura of white.

Then, suddenly, without warning, the body of light quickly broke free of the waters of the lake. It hung before us for a moment before breaking off into separate glowing trails once more, which in unison rose quickly and silently into the night sky. All too quickly the trails of light were gone, and all at the lake was silent and dark.

✣

The next morning, while we packed, Jasmine and I exchanged theories as to what we had witnessed the previous night.

"I think we relived the moment that the village flooded," began Jasmine, her tone assured and confident. "We heard the bells… which would have been the warning sign, like in the stories, but we experienced much more. We heard the rush of the water…and I think—you shall call me foolish, but I think we saw the release of the villagers' souls. I think we saw them depart for heaven."

Smiling and impressed at her theory, I felt it impossible to find fault. It made as much sense to me as any. I believed we had experienced a common type of haunting whereby a traumatic event, such is its impact on time and space, is imprinted on its surroundings, replaying time and again to the unfortunate and terrified few who might find themselves caught within its influence. Of course, this was but a theory (though I would investigate many more cases that would provide further evidence to support it), and I would present it as such, crediting Lady Fawksby equally for her ideas, when relaying my findings to the professor and his students.

✣

Our goodbye was one of awkward touch and fumbled talk. Neither said to the other what was really on the tips of our tongues, though looking back, I would question whether we needed to. Jasmine returned to her dying husband and I to my cramped office. Neither of us knew the next time that we would meet, but each departed feeling closer to the other.

Twenty-One
THE DEATH OF A LORD

Burton Agnes, Yorkshire, November 1875

The envelope lay on my desk, neat and perfectly centred. The elegant handwriting, though immediately familiar to me, implied nothing of the sorrow contained within. I knew the purpose of the letter and its contents before opening the envelope—no, before touching the envelope. Is it possible that such a letter may hold the energies and emotions of the author? Feeling the cold air numb my fingertips as they hovered over the paper, at that moment, I would have agreed this to be so.

Lord Fawksby had passed away three days earlier. Taken during the night by an untreatable fever. Jasmine informed me that his passing had been peaceful.

I was required to attend the funeral.

Specifically, I was to stay at Burton Agnes Hall at the request of Jasmine. The rest of the letter consisted of the specifics of my stay. It was a perfunctory piece, and her grief was apparent, at least to me, not in what she said but in what she did not. I departed for Yorkshire later that afternoon.

❖

I was met by members of the hall's domestic staff, all of whom were attired suitably in black. None would raise their eyes to meet mine as they busied about their work. I could not decide whether this was a trait of legitimate mourning or whether, as funeral rites often called for, merely the actions of individuals playing their parts. It is true that Lord Fawksby had been well liked among his staff, and I entered the hall hoping that their grief was genuine.

My luggage was taken to my quarters, and I was instructed to enter the grand hall, where the body of Lord Fawksby lay, so that I might pay my respects. The coffin of Lord Fawksby lay in the centre of the hall and was adorned with flowers, keepsakes and wreaths of varying sizes and colours. A solitary mourner knelt beside the coffin, dressed in an ornate mourning dress. Jasmine's face was hidden from sight, courtesy of a black lace veil. She knelt still and silent. Aside from her and the two men by the doors, assigned by the church to keep a watchful eye on the corpse of the lord, the room was empty.

I approached Jasmine tentatively, my every step ringing out loudly across the emptiness of the hall. Reaching her, I paused. She did not look up; such was the requirement of the mourning ritual. A woman, it was said, was to mourn with dignity and passion, for hers was the duty of care in life and death. My hand hovered over her shoulder. I was unsure how to proceed. I desperately wanted to console her, to take her in my arms and help rid her of her sorrow, yet protocol and my respect for Jasmine meant that this was neither the time nor the place.

Instead, I stepped forwards and addressed the body of Lord Fawksby. I forget the exact words I used, though I afforded him a degree of unreserved respect. Fawksby was a good man, and though I was conflicted by his death, this was a man I held in high esteem. My final words to him outlined this, and upon taking my leave, I heard Jasmine begin to weep.

❖

I have said I felt a degree of conflict over the death of Lord Fawksby, and this was true, selfish though it might appear. I am but a man, flawed and imperfect. To recognise one's faults is to understand oneself, and with the benefit of years, I am able to do so now. It is true that I loved Jasmine, and I suspected she loved me in return. Let me be clear here; I did not see Lord Fawksby as an obstacle to our relationship. Jasmine was duty-bound to him by way of marriage, and though we had shared brief moments of high emotion together, not once did I make her marriage any of my business. Such was my love and admiration for Jasmine, seeing her loyalty only added to my adoration.

Still, with his passing, she was no longer bound to him. She had cared for her husband and remained faithful to her vows. I realised that a period of mourning would be required, and I vowed that I would make myself available to Jasmine as and when needed and not until. Did I feel guilty harbouring the feelings I had towards her? I will admit that sometimes I did. But I would counter that the heart wants what the heart wants, and as of yet our actions had hurt no one but ourselves. Jasmine would grieve her husband and, in time, would look to return to life anew. Whether we would resume our friendship was in the hands of fate. All I could do was support her through this difficult time, if that was to be what she wished.

❖

St Martin's Church lay in the grounds of Burton Agnes Hall. Those who had travelled to mark the passing of Lord Fawksby far outnumbered the seats the small church held, and a great many mourners (myself included) found themselves standing outside.

The funeral procession passed by us, and Jasmine, her face still hidden from view, saw me standing at the side of the path and motioned that I stand by her side. I could hear the mutters of disapproval coming from the crowd as I took my place next to her. Did I care? Not for a moment. The way I saw it was that Jasmine required my presence during this difficult time. Though it was not proper practice to call upon the aid of another during a period of mourning, and indeed many assembled did criticise her actions in the years that followed, I stood true to my principles. Jasmine needed my support and I gave it unequivocally.

As the funeral service drew to a close and the coffin of Lord Fawksby was taken from the foot of the altar to be laid in his family mausoleum, I felt a strong hand grasp my forearm. I placed my arm around Jasmine's shoulder, much as I had done on the banks of Wastwater a few months earlier. She turned towards me, shaking and overcome with grief. I whispered to her that I would be here for her, no matter what fate may dictate. She placed her forehead on my chest and began to weep.

❖

There is little else of note left to say regarding the matter of the funeral. Lord Fawksby was interred in the crypt which bore his family name and the rest of the day was spent in polite conversation with assorted mourners. Lord Fawksby, it seemed, had been held in high esteem, and so was his widow. Speaking of Jasmine, I maintained a respectable distance for the remainder of the afternoon. It would not do to draw attention to our friendship and encourage disparaging remarks on this of all days. I observed her from afar as she spoke to each mourner in turn. How my heart longed to ease her suffering! Seeing those we love endure pain is the cruelest of life's tests. Unable to do as much, I at least felt satisfied that I had afforded her some form of comfort. My needs were of no importance.

The next morning, Jasmine, I was informed, had confined herself to her quarters and did not wish to be disturbed. I understood. The effort of the previous day had likely left her drained. Abandoning her to be alone with her grief was one of the most difficult moments of my life. Every instinct called for me to remain behind so that I might offer her support. This, I quickly recognised, was my own selfish desire.

I departed later that morning. I wished not to intrude upon her further. She knew where I was should she be in need of my presence.

Twenty-Two

THE HAUNTING OF FENTON HOUSE

Hampstead, London, January 1876

It was Lady Gracefirth who sought me out whilst attending the funeral of Lord Fawksby and not the other way around. I had no intention of discussing my work nor my experiences, as it was neither the time nor the place, but it seemed my reputation preceded me, and against the will of the beleaguered Lord Gracefirth, I was privy to a series of incidents which tarnished the reputation of Fenton House whether I wished it or not.

The lady informed me that their home had become known in the city of London as one rife with hauntings. Indeed, the notoriety of Fenton House kept all but the staunchest of souls from visiting and was causing considerable harm to the standing of Lord and Lady Gracefirth. This caused the lady a great degree of distress, and she was on the verge of tears as she informed me of the failure of several recent dinner parties. Guests refused to stay the night and often left before the serving of the main course; such was the ferocity of the haunting. One bedroom on the second floor had been sealed for a number of years. None of the household staff would set foot in the room after a particular incident one morning, the details of which caused Lady Gracefirth to break down further whilst attempting to enlighten me.

To alleviate her stress (and to prevent drawing further attention, this was a funeral and a particular behaviour was to be expected of its guests), I assured her that I would visit in the new year with the intention of staying at Fenton House until the cause of her anguish and of the mysterious disturbances which plagued her home was isolated and explained.

With my mind fixed firmly on Jasmine and the occasion of the funeral, I admit that I gave little thought as to who or what might be manifesting within Fenton House, and come the new year, I foolishly approached the investigation ill prepared. It was a mistake that I would endeavour not to make again.

❖

A former merchant's house, characteristic of the seventeenth century, Fenton had passed through the hands of various family lines, all of which had suffered bad fortune of one kind or another upon coming into ownership of the property. With such a chequered past, tales of a curse abounded, the most popular of which related to the original owner, Percival Manstrum.

Percival was one of a collection of merchants who first brought tea to the United Kingdom. Such was the demand for the drink in high society, his profits soared quickly, and he commissioned Fenton House to be built as his home.

There were, however, many who grew jealous of his newfound wealth, and one such business associate, a trader by the name of Frederick Bistole, was said to have made demands upon Manstrum and his business. When Manstrum defied Bistole, so went the tale, Manstrum's youngest son Elliot, who was aged seven at the time, was kidnapped by Bistole's men, and when Manstrum refused to pay the asking price for the release of his son, Bistole's men murdered him and dumped his body into the Thames.

Distraught at the loss of his child but defiant in the face of those who would see him ruined, Manstrum ordered work to continue on Fenton House, which he regarded as his legacy. However, with an influx of tea now flooding the country, his initial monopoly on the market faltered, and his profits soon fell. With the completion of the house having sapped all of his savings, his wife Esme left him, taking their surviving son Eldritch with her.

Wracked with guilt, Manstrum hanged himself from the balcony overlooking the great staircase. The seeds of the troubled history of Fenton House were sown.

No owner who followed could escape the bad fortune associated with the property. Some sold up after spending only a few months as owners; others fell ill and died under unexplained circumstances. One committed murder, another suicide. Several went mad and were incarcerated in Bethlem, Southwark. Now, it seemed, was the turn of Lord and Lady Gracefirth to suffer.

✣

"He's not well," said Lady Gracefirth as I bent to shake the hand of the seated lord. "He hasn't been for a while."

Lord Gracefirth sat in a tall-backed armchair by a large, ornate open fireplace. A red woollen blanket lay across his lap. I introduced myself and my intention. Not once did he turn his attention from the flames of the fireplace, which in spite of burning fiercely, made no impact upon the freezing climate of the room.

"He just stares at the fire or stares out of the window…I can't get a word from him. Nobody can!" continued Lady Gracefirth. "This place shall be the death of him, I swear!"

I assured her it wouldn't and that every effort would be taken to ascertain the cause of the disturbances that plagued Fenton House.

"I certainly hope that is the case, Mr Whyte," said Lady Gracefirth after she had outlined the history of their troubles. "For I fear the worst. They said this place was cursed when we purchased it. That might explain why we paid so little for it in the first place. Be that as it may, I am not willing for either my husband or me to fall victim to its torment."

✣

As I walked the grounds of Fenton House, not once did I feel at ease. The gardens, though designed and maintained to a high standard of care, afforded me not one moment of relaxation, so unable was I to shake the feeling that I was being observed by unseen eyes.

The house held similar vibrations. I experienced several cold spots where there ought to have been none and heard steady footsteps following after my own, only to turn to confront the individual so keen to follow in my wake but find no one there. The kitchen in particular held an uncomfortable air, though I am sure that I was the only person aware of the rancid stench of rotten meat that blanketed the scent of whatever meal the cook and his staff were preparing. I left the room after a short time with my nose pinched and my stomach turning. It was all I could do to stop myself from vomiting. Judging by the manner of ease in which the kitchen staff went about their duties, I can only assume that they either had no sense of smell or had become so used to the odour as to tolerate it with ease.

 I was required to ask one of the maids to show me to the infamous second-floor bedroom, as the entrance to the entire floor had been locked several months previously. Lord and Lady Gracefirth had turned over the floor to whatever evil manifested within the walls of Fenton House (the lady's words, not mine) and refused to even set foot on the staircase which led up to the second floor. It took most of the afternoon to source a member of the house staff bold enough first to request the key from Lady Gracefirth (who, in turn, kept it locked away in a location known only to her) and second to lead me into the bedroom that I should call my own that night.

 Upon setting foot inside, it was apparent that I would find little in the way of rest unless I first dedicated a large part of the evening to the cleaning of the room. A carpet of dust covered every surface and a number of cobwebs hung between bedpost, wall, window and wardrobe.

 "The room is untouched since the stay of the last guest, a Master Mark Fallows," said the maid, who despite the warnings from her seniors had volunteered to accompany me to my room. "We found him the next morning over by the pond," she continued, pointing out of the window towards the far corner of the grounds as she did so. "He wore only his night robe. Cook said he was blue when they found him. Talk is he got ill. Had to stay in the hospital for a while. The lady locked the room up after that. We are the first up here since. I hope you don't scare easy, mister?"

❖

Exhausted from cleaning the bedroom, I had fallen eventually asleep only to awake minutes later. It was not the cold that woke me, nor was it the persistent slamming of doors which had plagued my stay from the moment I had laid my head upon the pillow. No, again it was that peculiar sensation of being watched. Once one is of the mindset that one's every move, one's every breath, is under the scrutiny of another, it is all but impossible to put such ideas from one's thoughts.

 I sat upright and began to cough, my sudden movement having disturbed the layer of dust which had gathered upon the bed covers. I had left the curtains thrown back so that I might not suffer the torment of the bedroom in total darkness, for the night held court to a full moon and the room was bathed in a dull white light. Pressed against the window was a face, an impossible face at that. The face of a young boy, his throat slit, his neck open and rotting, his mouth twisted into an inhuman grin. The face at the window regarded me with hollow eyes. He watched me as I sat still and afraid, daring not to move, not even to breathe, as I stared back at him. Need I remind you that my bedroom was on the second floor.

 I gathered myself, still under the watchful gaze of the apparition, finding my slippers by my bedside and sliding my feet into them. I stood and turned to face the boy again. His smirk widened as I took a step towards the window. First one. Then another. The boy did not move. He watched intently as I neared him, his smirk developing a curious tilt.

I reached the window. Our eyes remained locked. From my vantage point, I could observe the rest of his features. He was a small child, dressed in a torn and ragged, water-stained nightshirt. I guessed his appearance to resemble that of a six- or seven-year-old boy. We stood facing one another, separated only by a thin pane of glass, each gaining the measure of the other. My heart thundered in my chest and the cold of the night numbed my extremities. It was his presence which chilled the air, of that I have no doubt. We remained stood before one another, neither willing to yield and flee, until suddenly, the boy opened his mouth inhumanly wide. I testify that it looked as though his jaw became dislocated, or would have, had the boy been of flesh and blood—such was the terrible angle at which the jaw hung. There came forth that same rancid stench I had experienced in the kitchen, and I felt suddenly unsteady and nauseous. A high-pitched wail filled the air, shaking the glass in the window frame, as the boy slowly began to descend, down further past the first floor, until he disappeared into the ground beneath me. It was then I realised my room was situated above the kitchens.

✣

I explained over breakfast the next morning my encounter with the apparition of the boy. I mentioned that the odour I had faced during our meeting was one and the same as the stench I had noted in the kitchen earlier that day. (Funnily enough, no other member of the household would admit to having experienced that odour, which led me to believe it existed on a separate plane to our existence, one perhaps accessible only to the supernaturally gifted.) I suggested that the floor of the kitchen and the neighbouring grounds be pulled up. My theory was that I had met the apparition of the merchant's son, and that the body of this poor wretch lay interred somewhere beneath the manor house, likely nearby to where I had seen his apparition submerge itself, and that the resultant haunting may well have been a plea for a proper burial.

❖

I left Lord and Lady Gracefirth in good spirit, for the advice that I had imparted, I was promised, was to be acted upon. True to their word, I received notice a few weeks later that the crumbled skeletal remains of a young child had been unearthed beneath the kitchen floor. As per my instructions, the bones were transferred to a nearby cemetery, and a Catholic burial followed.

There have been no more reported disturbances at Fenton House since the burial. Indeed, Lord Gracefirth was freed of his mysterious stupor and lived to the age of ninety-four. Lady Gracefirth elected not to stay in Fenton House after the death of her husband, citing that it was too grand a home to dwell within alone. The property is now owned by a distinguished botanist.

Twenty-Three

THE MAN WHO DID NOT DIE

Dersingham, King's Lynn, Norfolk, February 1876

Death has a season; of that I am sure. During the months of November through March, when the nights seem to run cold and uninterrupted, death works tirelessly to take those we love from us. I have seen a definite pattern. My parents passed in December and January respectively, barely a year apart. Lord Fawksby passed in November, and more than I care to mention have succumbed to death's touch during those long winter months. Perhaps it is then that the spirit ails most, the absent sun unable to give strength and hope to those who have given in to the fatigue brought about by age and sickness? Perhaps ill luck runs freely in the cold and the dark? Though I see patterns and I venture theories, I cannot prove a season of death as such. I just know it to be true.

Which is why it seemed natural to receive a letter in the winter of 1876 on the matter of death, or should I say deaths, with regard to one man. Perplexed? I am sure you are, as was I. Puzzled further were the family of Joshua Roberts and the parish of Dersingham, who, having mourned the passing of Mr Roberts, had buried him in the grounds of St Nicholas's three times over. The reason for this letter? Mr Roberts, fearing being buried alive yet again and having heard of my reputation, indicated that should his death be suspected once more, I was to be sent for immediately so that I and only I may ascertain whether he had truly passed away.

Of course, I could understand Mr Roberts's fear of being buried alive. After all, who would want to wake in a cramped, dark box, with no room to move and only a few minutes of air with which to breathe? Your cries and bangs unheeded, muffled by the damp earth. Your grieving loved ones standing above, oblivious to your torment. Not I, that is for sure—but to be declared dead and then buried three times? Either the village physician was vastly unqualified or something was seriously amiss with the physiology of Joshua Roberts.

✣

I was greeted at the door to the family home by Frances Roberts, Joshua's long-suffering wife. She was a frail woman of middle age. She stood with a stoop, and dark shadows circled her eyes. She ushered me inside and instructed me to sit. A small fire burned in the fireplace. There was one other person in the room. He was a young fellow, well dressed, though he looked a tad out of sorts. I later discovered that was due to my presence.

"Doctor Monroe," said the man without standing. We made brief eye contact as I sat before he turned his attention to the fireplace. "Honestly, I see no need for your presence…"

"He said he wanted him here, said him by name, should this happen again," said Frances from over my shoulder. "We only just got him out last time, he was purple for God's—" Frances paused, suddenly ashamed. "Forgive me, I forget myself sometimes."

I assured her that there was nothing to forgive and settled back to listen to the account of the many deaths of Joshua Roberts.

"The first time," the doctor began, "we found him up in the north field. He'd collapsed over the plough. By the time I'd gotten to him, he was cold and stiff."

"But he weren't dead," interrupted Frances as she set a kettle of water on the small stove located at the rear of the room.

"To all appearances he certainly looked so," snapped the doctor, his face flushed crimson. "He had no pulse, you understand, and he was cold as death—I've been around enough corpses to know how they feel to the fingertips."

"Yes, but he weren't," said Frances again.

"The body was kept in the home that night so that it might be washed in accordance with the usual funeral rites. We buried him the next morning."

"Tried to," chirped Frances, her back to both the doctor and me.

"We'd not added the lid yet. The family requested an open casket until the final moments of the service. He sat bolt upright mid-reading," continued Doctor Monroe. "Gave us all a fright. Poor Mrs Tanner, the organist, collapsed and hit her head on the keys. The dreadful note that the organ produced merely punctuated our horror!"

Frances stood between us, passing a cup of hot tea to each in turn. "He made a full recovery, though, didn't he. He'd used to joke that he was once dead but got better. How we laughed! Until it happened again, that is."

Doctor Monroe took a sip of his tea, placed it aside and leaned towards me. "The second time, it happened upstairs."

"We were in bed," interrupted Frances again. "He's normally such a fusspot, always tossing and turning, but he hadn't moved a muscle in hours. 'Course, I couldn't sleep, because I knew something was amiss. I spoke to him a few times, but he didn't answer. He can be like that, though, most men are. So I gave him a shove. He was cold as ice! I threw open the curtains and he was lying there, stiff as a board, his eyes agog staring straight up at the ceiling. 'Course, I screamed. Screamed the bloody place down! The doctor came by a while later, after I'd calmed a little."

I turned to the doctor, who had returned his attention to his drink. "Same thing again," he said. "No pulse, cold, early-onset rigor mortis. He was dead. I was sure."

"We cleaned him up and kept him here two days this time," continued Frances as she returned to her duties by the stove. "Oh, he went a terrible blue colour, and his head seemed to swell. It didn't look like Josh when we took him to the church."

"This time, we got as far as lowering him into the ground," said Doctor Monroe. "The priest was delivering his final blessing when the knocking began."

"Don't misunderstand me," said Frances as she washed dishes in the sink, "it was still a shock to us all that he wasn't dead, but less so…if you can understand that?"

I nodded and said that I did.

"The third time, we'd actually started to bury him," said the doctor, finishing his drink.

"We got him out. He really did nearly die that time!"

"Again, all the same symptoms. In fact," said the doctor as he moved to stand, "come with me."

❖

Joshua Roberts lay stiff and still, looking to all intents and purposes deceased. I placed my thumb and forefinger either side of his throat and searched for a pulse. After a time, I withdrew my hand, unable to locate one.

"See?" said Doctor Monroe with a smirk. "He seems dead, doesn't he? Look at his complexion. Feel his skin."

I did as I was instructed. Joshua looked swollen and bloated. Blue veins lay pronounced beneath the surface of his yellowed skin. He was cold to the touch, and his flesh was tough and malleable. I enquired as to how long he had appeared this way.

"Two days now, almost three," answered the doctor. "I'm almost convinced he is actually dead this time…can you not smell him?"

It was true that there was an unpleasant smell of defecation which hung in the air (not that was ever a proof of death), yet I had but one test to conduct, one that had served me well previously. I took a small mirror from my carry case and placed it beneath Joshua's nostrils.

For a long time, nothing happened, and I could sense the growing certainty of conviction emanating from Doctor Monroe, until, faint though it may have appeared at first, the mirror began to fog.

I showed this first to the doctor, who, flabbergasted, could only grunt in acknowledgement. Then I called for Frances and placed the mirror beneath the nostrils of her husband, and though the wait was long, the mirror did indeed fog again.

When she asked what it meant, it was the doctor who answered. "It is the sign of a breath taken. Though abnormally slowly, your husband *is* breathing. Therefore, he is alive."

Satisfied that my work was done, I left the mirror with the doctor, instructing him to use it if ever in doubt.

✧

Though I never did uncover a cause of the peculiar condition which afflicted Joshua Roberts, proving he was alive was all that had been required. Mr Roberts wrote to me upon his recovery to thank me for my time and diligence. He explained that my experiments had helped ease his fear of being buried alive, noting that the chances of such ought now to be lower for him than for most.

I can only surmise that he was in fact afflicted by some kind of sleeping sickness, one in which the body enters a state of almost complete death and the mind becomes unreachable. Indeed, Mr Roberts said to me in his correspondence that he had no recollection of his state, nor ever felt any lingering ill effect. Though most definitely a curious ailment, I consider this to be a mystery of the body rather than one of the paranormal. Still, a fascinating case all the same, and it leads me to wonder, just how many people are we burying who have been mistaken as dead?

Twenty-Four

THE MARK OF THE RIPPER

Whitechapel, London, September 1888

There was only one criminal investigation in which I partook; though I have been asked many times since to advise on more, I politely decline. Such was the impact of said case, I wished never to involve myself in the investigation of criminal activity again.

How can this be so? I hear you ask. *For is not the basis of your work grounded in the macabre?* Indeed, it is. However, I am no lawman, and coming face to face with England's most notorious murderer was enough to quell any interest I might have entertained in examining the motive of true crime.

It was August 1888 when the Whitechapel murderer first struck. By the ninth of September, Leather Apron (as he was referred to by police) had claimed his second victim. It was at this point that Detective Inspector Edmund Reid made contact in the hope that my experience in the field of the paranormal, specifically the occult, might shed light on who the perpetrator was of the grisly murders.

Reid was a dedicated sort, gifted much as I (though he would be loath to admit it) with the ability to pick at the threads of truth that others in his field might easily overlook. The Whitechapel murders, however, left him baffled. There were no witnesses, no apparent motive, and there were no clues left behind by the killer. The savagery of the deaths (Reid used the term *butchered* in his initial correspondence) appalled him the most. Used to dealing with crimes of sense and motive, something about this case spoke to his instinct on a level he could neither explain nor hope to understand. Having read of my exploits and with London in the grip of hysteria, he summoned me to Scotland Yard.

It was well known that all of the victims were suspected of working as prostitutes, and theories abounded as to why Jack the Ripper (as the media referred to him) targeted only prostitutes. I heard many an interesting debate about why this might be, but my own instinct told me that they were killed because they were easy targets. Prostitutes walked the notoriously dangerous London streets alone and would often disappear into seclusion with men they did not know. This provided the Ripper with a relatively simple means of acquiring his prey, and though I voiced my opinion loudly, it fell upon largely deaf ears.

As for the brutality of the murders, I could offer little in the way of an explanation. I ruled out sacrificial motivation due to the ferocity of the attacks and the wounds inflicted, arguing that a sacrificial or occult-driven kill would appear altogether less frenzied. The kill itself was not the motivation in such a ritual, only the release of the soul or the harvesting of an organ or body part. In the Ripper killings, the wounds inflicted upon the bodies of the women indicated a man in the throes of anger and release.

Reid thanked me for my insight and assured me that my theories would be given further discussion. Feeling that my trip to the nation's capital had been somewhat in vain, I elected to stay a while and see how the case played out.

☙

How I came to be in Dutfield's Yard during those early hours of Sunday the thirtieth of September I cannot say. Only that such was my fascination with the case of the Ripper that I found myself walking the streets of Whitechapel in an effort to capture him. Indeed, my exploits had seen me brought in for questioning several times, such was the rarity of a well-dressed man walking the streets of Whitechapel. Each time Reid explained who I was and what it was that I was doing, before taking me aside and advising that I might wish to return to Manchester or risk becoming a Ripper suspect.

Alas, I did not heed his words, for had I done so, perhaps my face would have remained unblemished.

I saw the woman later identified as Elizabeth Stride enter Dutfield's with a tall man just before one in the morning. What initially drew me to follow this particular fellow, whom I had spied earlier that same night, was his walk, or rather his lack of it. Allow me to explain. Here was a man dressed head to foot in black, his features hidden beneath a long coat which dragged along the sodden cobbles, his face beneath a tall hat which cast his eyes in shadow.

Oddly, the man had no noticeable gait. He seemed to glide along the street, though his feet were not visible due to the length of his coat. It was most unnatural. As was his height. Stooped, he stood at nearly six and a half feet. I tailed him for a half hour until he led Mrs Stride into the darkness of said alleyway.

Following after her, I heard at first a cry, followed by the splash of liquid upon stone. Rounding the corner, I saw it (for *him* would be entirely the wrong word to describe the beast) standing over Mrs Stride's prone body. Her throat was open, the wound broad and red. Blood pumped in powerful arcs from the tear in her neck. It stood over her, blade unfurled, hovering above her abdomen, a frenzied look in its eyes.

I must have gasped or made some utterance in reaction to the scene before me, for its attention shifted from the body of Mrs Stride and onto me. It stood fully erect, shedding the coat which hid its grotesque, inhuman features from the world. The thing that was the Ripper spoke to me. *"Audes me perturbare?"* I later learned this was Latin for "you dare disturb me?"

In a bid to draw attention to the scene of the murder and my dangerous predicament, I began to yell. The demon (I have no other name for a creature with elongated limbs, scarlet-tinged skin, inhuman height and curved blades set as claws) advanced upon me. I stumbled backwards, falling onto my rear at the precise moment the creature swung its talons towards me. A searing pain exploded in my face and I felt the sting of hot blood enter my eyes. With my hands raised above me in pitiful defence and blind to my attacker, I awaited the final blow. It never came.

❖

An officer of the law helped me to my feet. His young colleague rested his palms against the wall opposite, bent double, and vomited at the sight of the dead woman. The drizzle clung to our skin, coating the insides of our lungs. I'll always remember the smell of that alleyway: copper and bile.

❖

Later that night, the Ripper claimed another victim. Catherine Eddowes was found butchered in Mitre Square, not long after the officers had arrived at the scene where I lay with Mrs Stride. Eddowes' body was subject to severe mutilation. It seems that though I had indeed interrupted the Ripper at work, his bloodlust had not yet been satiated.

❖

The death of Catherine Eddowes occurred because of my shortcomings, of that I am certain. I placed myself amidst a situation I had no right to meddle in. Again, naivety and arrogance blinded me, and though I had the best intentions at heart, another innocent woman was slain. I had interrupted the killer and his ritual. The murder of Mrs Stride, for whatever reason, did not satisfy his need that night. Driven by a madness likely unfathomable to man, the demon's need to mutilate, to harvest both flesh and organ, though disturbed by my foolish intrusion, led him to kill again and quickly.

Many times I have anguished over the events of that night, and though it pains me to admit, if I had resisted following the Ripper and his prey into that alley, it is likely that Eddowes would have survived that night. Did I really think I could save Stride from the clutches of the Ripper? Is that why I followed after her? I shall be honest here, for this is the purpose of this book. My curiosity meant that I had to follow. I had no plan to save the woman, though of course a part of me hoped I might formulate one in haste, once having been sure as to the predicament in which she found herself.

Alas, this was not to be.

I panicked.

Having set eyes upon the monstrosity that stood over her corpse, all rational thought, all bravado, all confidence in my abilities bled out from my being as quickly as Mrs Stride had emptied of her blood on to those cold, damp cobblestones. I was the boy who swung helplessly from the branch of the old oak in Alverton again. Reckless, naïve and in over my head. My fate lay in the hands of another and again I was fortunate to escape with my life.

Regrettably, Catherine Eddowes was not. Her name is forever embedded in the list of mistakes that I torture myself with daily.

I mentioned earlier that this was the first and last criminal investigation in which my services were utilised. The reasons for this are simple. Where before I had blood on my hands (such as with Nathaniel the vampyre child and the creatures of Woolpit), though regretful of the outcome of those investigations, I came away from the experiences seeing the error of my ways. Errors can be mended, and so long as you learn from them, better yourself because of them, there is always a chance of redemption.

When faced with the Ripper, a manner of creature that I shall never be able to comprehend, I realised that on reflection I had no idea what I would have done differently, nor what I would do if faced with a similar situation in the future. It is important to recognise the signs life has a habit of placing before us (sometimes right beneath our noses) that can somehow easily be missed. Not knowing how I would correct my mistake that night, not knowing how I might have been able to save either one or both of those women, told me that I was not intended to use my abilities for the solving of crime.

It took a great many months of sorrow and reflection to arrive at that conclusion. However, I am a stout believer that if we are to truly know ourselves, we must constantly ask ourselves the questions which we knowingly shy away from, the answers to which, though difficult to understand, difficult even to admit to, ultimately set us free from any burden of guilt or self-doubt.

✣

To this day, I wear the mark of the Ripper upon me, and when I am asked about the origins of the scar which runs from the left corner of my mouth up across my eye before coming to an end on my forehead, many dispute my claim. The scar is a constant reminder of my shortcomings that night. The Whitechapel murderer was never apprehended. Nor did Inspector Reid and his associates believe my description of the killer. They claimed panic and confusion clouded my account, brought about by the ordeal of my attack and having witnessed the murder of Mrs Stride. I know this not to be true, for I have seen the evils of this world and I have looked into the eyes of the Ripper.

Twenty-Five

THE MAN I BECAME

Home, June 1914

A sure sign of old age is the ever-encroaching presence of death. If fate smiles upon you and grants you a fair run of years, then first he shall come for your parents, the loss of whom is undoubtedly meant as one of life's stubborner tests. My father passed in 1894 and my mother soon after. With her dying breath, she told me not to grieve her, for it was merely her time and she was looking forward to meeting Victoria and Father again. Of course, grief is a necessary reaction. One cannot move forwards until the process is all but complete.

Death shall then come for your peers and your colleagues, none of whom you ever thought of as old. The feeling upon hearing news of their passing is always the same, one of shock dashed with a touch of fear. If so-and-so has passed, then who might be next? *Could it soon be that my friends hear of my passing away?* The death of others has a nasty habit of raising the question of one's own mortality.

I have attended countless funerals these past few years, and I have paid my final respects to many a treasured friend. The nature of my work afforded me the luxury of both travel and extended correspondence. I have met a great number of people during my work, many of whom I remain in contact with. I am blessed with friendship much as I am blessed in other ways.

Back to the issue of funerals. They are ghastly affairs. One never grows accustomed to their attendance and protocol. The one saving grace is that I shall not be present at mine!

Writing my memoirs has afforded me ample time for reflection. Flicking through the pages, I can see how I have developed into a man of character. I am a firm believer that our experiences mould us. I see us born unto the world much as a piece of fresh clay is placed on the potter's wheel. The clay has the potential to become anything that the potter desires, and through his hands, a pot, vase, ashtray or any number of items are formed. The potter's hands are the experiences that we encounter during our lifetimes, and we are the clay. We are shaped accordingly but—and here is a crucial difference—we are not inert like clay. We can choose to a degree how to react to our experiences, and in doing so, choose how we are shaped.

This is the way I see my character as having developed. I was once young, reckless and wet behind the ears. I was a boy in a man's shoes. I made mistakes, dozens of them, many not mentioned here that shall perhaps be recorded in a further volume, but mistakes all the same.

Now, I am wiser, ever cynical to those who only regard me in passing, but with eyes wide open and a mind ready to accept anything should I be able to find tangible proof.

The knowledge I have gained from the years I spent investigating the paranormal I pass to you now. You will find it hidden in plain sight within these pages. There are several young men I have mentored in the field of paranormal investigation in recent years, and I am proud to say that they have gone on to not only further the foundations of my work, but to better it.

I set out to define a legacy for myself, and I admit that my reasons were largely self-serving. But now, in my twilight years, I realise that a legacy only lives on if it is passed from generation to generation, much like many of the folk tales I have dedicated my life to investigating.

For a long time, I believed that the sole purpose of life was to undertake a journey of loss, for loss is inevitable, death is inevitable. No longer do I believe this to be so, for while we shall all live, love and lose, life is not measured by the number of tears shed or hours grieved, it is measured in the number of hearts touched and moments of happiness shared. The journey of life encompasses all, the difficult times as well as those of elation. The character we take to the grave is the sum of all of those experiences. Does that character live on in another time or another place? I do not have proof as such to provide a definitive answer, though no longer do I fear to find out for myself.

There are other stories to share with you, but they shall have to remain with me for now, for the hour is late and Jasmine calls.

ABOUT THE Author

Award-winning author, Dan Weatherer, was first published by *Haunted Magazine* in Spring, 2013 and followed this with a collection of short stories titled *The Soul That Screamed* (Winner of the Preditors & Editors™ Readers' Poll 'Best Anthology 2013'). A further two collections *Only the Good Burn Bright* (2015, James Ward Kirk Fiction) and *Neverlight*—shortlisted for the first annual Arnold Bennett Literary Prize—(2016, Spectral Press) quickly followed. His first non-fiction book titled *What Dwells Within* was released in 2015 detailing the life's work of paranormal investigator Jayne Harris.

His fourth collection *Just Eventide*, was released in 2017, along with historical novella, *Crippen*, (Spectral Press).

An accomplished playwright, Dan was winner of the 2017 Soundwork UK play competition, a finalist in the Blackshaw

Showcase Award 2016, and a two-time finalist of the Congleton Players One Act Festival, 2016. *The Dead Stage*, a book detailing Dan's experiences as a novice playwright, was published courtesy of Crystal Lake Publishing in October, 2018

In 2015, Dan was shortlisted for the prestigious position of Staffordshire Poet Laureate 2016-2018 and in 2019, was nominated for a local Heroes award (The Sentinel) for his continued promotion of literacy and mental health issues in the city of Stoke on Trent.

Dan lives in Staffordshire with his wife Jenni and is a (proud) full-time dad to his daughter Bethany, and son Nathan.